Change of Tides

The Unspoken Heart Series

Amy Astorga

Change of Tides
The Unspoken Heart Series

ISBN 9780996156226

Scripture taken from the New King James Version®. Copyright © 1982 by Thomas Nelson. Used by permission. All rights reserved.

Cover design by Story Graphix Plus
Interior design by Kimberly Martin of Jera Publishing
Copy editing by Natalie Jean Astorga and Emmanuel Alonso Astorga

*For my mother who was there in the beginning,
and for my husband who will be there until the end.*

"Greater love has no one than this; that a man lay down his life for his friends."

John 15:13 NKJV

Chapter One

The tide pulled back from the shadowed sand, leaving a creamy white sheet of glittering foam. My arms propped my body up from the pebbled ground just high enough to rest on both elbows. I looked down at my tail that glistened in the moonlight and gave a cry of despair.

This wasn't real.

It couldn't be. This heavy fish's appendage that descended from my waist wasn't right. It wasn't natural. I was supposed to see legs kick with a thought, not one muscle. How was I supposed to swim? The pulse in my neck swelled hot at the thought.

The voice of Avangeline drove fear even deeper, "You better keep quiet when your friends arrive! Unless you want to be on the front page of every newspaper, I suggest you keep your mouth shut!" Her harsh words were both a plea and a command. My presence at her murder posed an unforeseen predicament. She didn't plan for me to witness Ryan's death. Her whole transformation was calculated. She didn't anticipate I would hide in the cleft of the rocks and watch her transgression play out. Avangeline needed to cover her tracks and get rid of me fast—even if it meant dragging my body to the shore herself.

Another wave came in, spilling water toward her newly acquired feet. She turned on her heel and ran up the hill.

I glanced at the silhouette that loomed near the rocks and swallowed the lump in my throat. Marcus remained motionless as Avangeline joined his side. I needed his help. I needed something. Anything. I needed a solution. I needed a savior to come and rescue me from this watery hell that was to be my future. But I received nothing. He didn't even look in my direction.

"Gwendolyn? Ryan? Are you there? Gwendolyn?" The voices of Joey and Jessica grew louder. My friends didn't know what happened. They were expecting to find Ryan holding me under the stars. They had no idea I was a mermaid and Ryan disintegrated into a pile of ash. The shock of his murder would be parallel to my form.

The thunderous clap of a large wave sounded, and my waist became submerged. For one suffocating moment, I considered a horrifying option. I could drag myself up the shore and flag down Joey and Jessica. I could get their attention by waving my arms and explain all that happened after the party. They would marvel at my appearance and ask a million questions, but they would never accept the reason why I transformed. Their sympathy for my misfortune would instantly become abhorrence.

"Ryan? Gwendolyn? Ryan . . . man, are you there?"

My soul fainted within me. With the utterance of a prayer, I filled my lungs with a thin breath of air and turned to face the ocean that waited. An incoming wave rose high above my head, swirling indigo peaks with white foam. A scream filled my throat as it struck me in the face and pushed me flat on my back.

I entered a world of total darkness.

The light from the moon was instantly smothered by a blanket of water that spread above my face. The thick, gritty current crashed down upon my chest, expelling the little remaining breath that I held. My pulse throbbed hard in my ears as I struggled to break through the ocean's churning surface. The merciless riptide grabbed my body like a ragdoll and sucked me deep into its trenches. Bits of shell and rock tore my skin like glass as I tumbled wildly in the darkness. I kicked at the water in a desperate attempt to swim, but a fish's tail responded to the command. My brain had not yet registered my transformation. A massive muscle pulled hard in my belly, spreading the delicate fins that were attached at its end. With a few strong flaps, I pushed through the rolling waters that collected at the shoreline and propelled straight to the top.

I burst through the surface with a sputtering gasp and fought to catch my breath. In my mind's eye I imagined two legs kicking vigorously in the water—only a greenish-gray tail waved steadily in their place. I ran one hand down the length of my abdomen and flinched. A seamless transition from skin to scale could be felt just above my hipline. The wide, flexing muscle was hard and slightly slippery, swaying with precise calculation to each mental kick. I pulled my hand away from my tail and continued to grope at the water. The confusion of my appendage was more than I could bear.

Acknowledgement of my aberration brought a flood of self-awareness and grief. I glanced in the direction of the shoreline, halfway expecting to see everyone watching me in horror. Marcus and Avangeline were engaged in a conversation with Joey and Jessica. Excuses for Ryan's and my absence would undoubtedly be made. Avangeline would ensure my friends stayed oblivious to our whereabouts. Little did Joey know the very stranger he spoke to was the one who took Ryan's life.

My skin prickled with gooseflesh, and I shuddered at the thought. I could have prevented his death. He was my best friend and my fiancé, yet I let him die without a struggle. So many memories we shared were completely obliterated by one single decision. And what was the motive for my reaction? Anger at his infidelity? Fear of Avangeline's retaliation? Doubt that he would die? I bit my lower lip and moaned in total abhorrence. It scared me to look into the depths of my heart. Not even I understood the choices I made.

I took another look at the conversing crowd and willed to disappear within the shadows. If Joey turned his head, he would find me floating out to sea. Suddenly, my perilous situation became even more complicated. I loathed swimming underwater as much as I hated my aquatic attachment, but I feared my discovery even more. I took in a reluctant deep breath and sank beneath the surface.

The warm water felt thick as I pulled apart its drapes. With a full moon shining brightly in the sky, a creation of infinite splendor was unveiled before me. Tapestries of dark emerald velvet stretched for as far as the eye could see. Its gentle-moving currents stirred up wisps of effervesce, gold and sparkling, as I swam within its wake. I kicked my tail in short bursts of energy to prevent from going too fast. Slowly, I snaked my way through an ocean that was filled with beauty, wonderment, and power. Clusters of black floating seaweed draped like willow branches from the water's swaying surface. A wave pulled and they opened their folds, revealing a network of tiny fish that twinkled in their lengths. I pushed past the tangle of jelly-like ribbons and drifted toward the moonlight. Although I was underwater for only a few seconds, my lungs were completely depleted of air. The desire to breathe suddenly exceeded the fear of being noticed. Without giving it a second thought, I gave my tail a hard flap and quickly made my climb.

I broke through the ocean's choppy surface and gulped desperately for oxygen. A cold wind blew hard across my face, making a deep breath of air difficult to take. I expanded my chest, but received little relief. My throat bulged, and I coughed. It felt as though my lungs were changing, constricting somehow, and becoming unbearably tight.

I smoothed back my hair that whipped across my face and looked toward the shore. Four small figures stood talking in the darkness. Their company was at a greater distance and had become harder to see. A thin wisp of cloud covered the moon, making distinguishing identities of individuals near impossible. But what I was able to see, I was grateful for. I hadn't traveled so far out that I lost touch of what I knew—lifeguard station twelve, my friends who sought my presence, GlenPoint Strip that led to home—my parents.

My parents!

I covered my mouth with my hand and bit down on my palm. My parents—oh, my parents! They would be worried for me by now! Surely the night's hour was well past my curfew. If sleep prevented them from detecting my absence, it would certainly be discovered in the morning. A simple party at the beach would become their worst nightmare. Calls to the police would be nothing more than failed attempts. They would comb the sands of GlenPoint Beach and never know I was there.

They would think I was dead.

I stifled a sob and blinked my eyes, sending two tears streaming down my cheeks. I would never see them again. My father's infectious laughter, my mother's warm embrace, the memories we made as a tight-knit family of three—all were gone in a blink of an eye. Everything I knew and loved was swallowed in an ocean of perpetual torment.

Another gust of wind blew and the air grew uncomfortably thin. The four individuals who lingered on the shoreline had suddenly dispersed to two. Although I felt excluded from their aloof inner circle, I didn't want them to leave. They were all I had left— the last remains of human interaction. My peace rested in the visual of two detached people. Be it Marcus and Avangeline or Joey and Jessica, I feared once they left GlenPoint Beach my sanity would be shaken to the core.

One of them turned in my direction.

I took in a wheezy breath and ducked underwater.

A hard-rolling wave crashed down upon my head, pushing me deeper than I expected. The moon's precious glow had once again vanished, shrouding me in a cloth that was as dreaded and as black as death. I needed to stay out of sight, and I wasn't sure how long. My lungs were already out of air. I fanned my tail with a thought of a kick and slowly treaded in place. The smooth stir of tide pulled my body where it wished as I succumbed to the will of the ocean. I extended my arms at my sides to gain better balance as I floated.

A slippery object brushed against my hand.

I kicked my tail with instinctual force and surged back to the top. I exploded out of the water with a gargled scream and pawed at the waves on the surface. My hand tangled in a spider web of seaweed, pulling the leathery bundle of vines close to my body. I pushed away the plant that wrapped around my arms and steadied my breathing to a pant. My frightening encounter was nothing more than vegetation. The draping clusters of greenery were surrounding me like a fortress of floating walls, making every move in the darkness an accidental run-in. The ocean was such a complex and unforgiving environment. I was fortunate I didn't come across a jellyfish or an eel. Heaven only knew what creatures hid within the depths.

A realization suddenly hit me that I hadn't thought of before. I felt my face drain of all color.

Sharks.

Beasts of vicious enormity dwelled within my living space. I was no longer a human who held power over my circumstances. I didn't have the capacity to get into a boat or swim to safety if danger unexpectedly arose. I didn't have lifeguards manning the shoreline and boundaries for which I knew not to cross. Every flap of my tail lured the monsters from the crevasses. I was vulnerable and exposed, and any movement I made put my life in danger.

My vision pulsed in sync with my heartbeat. With trembling hands, I cleared away the remaining seaweed that clung to my frame and squinted to get a better look at the shore. The last remains of my company had vanished. The sobering perspective their presence provided had abruptly become nonexistent.

All at once, fears crawled out of the rafters of my mind and lined up to be looked over and embraced—Ryan's death and my participation, family and friends whose lives would be shattered by my disappearance, the dangerous environment I was forced to call home, basic tools of life that were lost overnight. Where would I sleep? What would I eat? What would I wear? My naked breasts were just as hard to accept as anything else I had to deal with. The Gwendolyn Hart that once existed, died, and nothing could bring me back from a future that was destined for destruction. Nothing except . . .

Murder.

My soulless body required a sacrifice to receive legs. I needed to lure a man to fall in love with me and give me his life with a kiss. The solution was as frightening as it was cruel. And it wasn't a haste decision. The act needed to be performed slowly and methodically, and every second spent fulfilling my entrapment was a second given for moral reflection. In the end, it was my life for his—an exchange of unjust scales. My side would always weigh out lacking. I would lay in my bed of pillows and cotton sheets and remember the man whose life that it cost. The demons that tormented Marcus's contentment would eventually come knocking on my door. It was a visit I wasn't wanting to entertain.

An image Ryan suddenly conjured in my mind. His blue eyes were ablaze with excitement as he took in every inch of Avangeline. She questioned his fidelity, and he defended his intentions with a pledge of total devotion. After seeing that her victim was ready for the taking, she demanded for his affection with a kiss. He, being smitten with the goddess that beckoned, was only more than willing to oblige. She ran her fingers through his sandy brown hair while he caressed the middle of her back. Their mouths pressed willingly in unbridled desire before he discovered he was stuck and struggled to break free. His taut skin stretched wrinkly. His angular jaw sagged. Both legs wobbled at the knees and buckled. His young, muscular body became shriveled like an old man's as she sucked the very life out from him. He crumpled to the sand in a pile of ash and clothing just in time for a wave to wash him away. The man who ate from the fruit of my seduction would ultimately fall to the sand in eternal ruin.

I closed my eyes and blotted out the image that felt so very fresh. A fine mist of saltwater carried up from the waves, choking my breath that was becoming quite labored. For the first time I noticed how very little input and output my lungs were exchanging. Deep breaths of air felt restricted and lacked substance, and if I received any relief from my feeble efforts, they were entirely depleted the moment I sank underwater.

I opened my mouth as wide as I could and inhaled with a strenuous rasp. A burning pain shot across my chest, and I exploded in a crackling cough. The more I tried to catch my breath, the more the pain spread. I grabbed at my throat to keep from sputtering as my heart began to race.

I couldn't breathe.

No matter how hard I tried, my lungs couldn't fill with enough oxygen. The simple act of breathing that nourished me since birth had suddenly become inefficient. It was as if my body was rejecting the very substance it needed and was requiring something different to live.

A hard-pressing wind beat across the ocean, splashing a wave against my face. I looked at the water that played quietly in the darkness and closed my eyes in despair. My oxygen wasn't coming from the right source. If my legs changed to a fish's tail, it would only make sense that my lungs changed as well. I needed to take a deep breath underwater.

The fiery pain that lingered in my chest spread to the middle of my back. I bent my head toward the glassy black water and lightly touched my lips to its surface. The ocean lapped against my mouth, whispering for me to breathe it in. I made a mental count of three and gave a sharp slurp. A flood of salty liquid shot down the back of my throat, and I gagged at the offering. I could taste blood. My failed attempt to remain alive offered no promise. White dots floated across my vision, and my ears began to ring. The night's starry sky that stretched above my head blended with the innumerable floating spots around me.

I needed to go home.

My sight darkened to black. I turned in the direction of the shore and fanned my tail with the little strength I had left. If I hurried, I could make it back before breakfast. I could drag myself up the shore and wait for someone to see me. They could carry me to their car and drive me back home. Yes! That was my plan. My parents would be so happy to see me that they would embrace my new body. I flapped my tail hard at the thought of their smiling faces and swam as fast as I could. I needed to make haste if I was going to make it back in time.

I just need to go home.

A thick object wrapped around my neck and pulled me underwater.

"Speak your name before I kill you!"

Chapter Two

"*I won't help you take her to the ocean. Let her future determine itself.*"

Avangeline's face twisted in expected rage. "*But I may be questioned for Ryan's death. Don't you care about that? Or are you afraid your beloved will have to face her fate? Forget about her, Marcus! She doesn't love you. I should've killed her when I had the chance.*"

I gave her a stare that pinned her to the ground and told her I wasn't amused. She knew not to overstep her boundaries. Although she was aggressive toward humans and insensitive to my failed relationship, there were lines she knew not to cross. Her fear of my wrath was greater than any spiteful vengeance.

"Fine!" she barked. "I don't need your help anyways. I can take care of her myself. Oh, stop trying to run away, Gwendolyn! It will only make your tail flap harder." She bent over the mermaid, who was overcome with terror, and dragged her unwilling body out to the shore. The image of Gwendolyn falling face-first to the sand was an image I would fight hard to forget. She disappeared in a wave of sweeping foam just in time to be concealed from the approaching visitors.

"Gwendolyn? Ryan? Where are you guys?" A couple appeared over the dune. They looked to each other in mutual bewilderment, obviously surprised to see us and not the friends they sought in concern.

I glanced at Avangeline, who ran to my side, and smirked at her ironic twist of fate. The savage beast who answered to no one in the ocean suddenly needed to be held accountable for her actions. She hadn't even been out of the water for an hour and was already being put on trial. She cursed under her breath and quickly wove her arm around mine. Although her affection was merely for show, I knew there was a measure of truth behind her actions. Her grip on my arm tightened as the pair approached.

"Uh . . . hey, guys. We don't mean to cram your space or anything, but have you seen a couple pass through here recently?" The young male with the red and blue braids spoke first.

"A couple? I haven't seen any couple. Have you seen anyone, sweetie?" Avangeline looked to me to respond. After she saw I wasn't going to help her in her facade, she shook her head promptly and said, "No, I'm sorry. We haven't seen anybody pass through here tonight. Why? Is there something we can help you with?"

"Well, sort of," the female answered. "We thought we heard our friend screaming for help a few minutes ago. She was looking for her fiancé, and his truck is still in the parking lot. We thought she may be in trouble."

Avangeline's skin grew clammy. She dropped my arm with nervous energy and thrust her hands in the front pouch of her sweatshirt. "Did you say you heard screaming?" she asked. "Oh, I'm sorry to have worried you. That was me screaming for help. My boyfriend and I were playing near the water, and he pushed me in. He knows how I hate getting wet, and yet, he still finds it amusing to torture me. You never cease to amaze me, Tristan."

Out of the corner of my eye, I saw Avangeline look for my contribution. My stare remained fixed on the guests before me. The couple drank in her lie like a cold glass of water. They looked to each other in silent relief and nodded.

After Avangeline saw she was in the clear, she finished her masterpiece with a brushstroke of humanity. "Anyways, I'll be sure to tell your friends you're looking for them. And, by the way, what are their names in case we come across them?"

"Their names are Ryan and Gwendolyn," the male informed. "Ryan is tall with light brown hair and a black shirt. And Gwendolyn has long blond hair. I think she's wearing an orange strapless dress. Isn't that right, Jess?" He looked to his companion who agreed with him. "Yes, it's orange. If you happen to see them, please have them give us a call. And, hey, sorry to have bothered you." He gave Avangeline a sheepish grin and quickly scanned her body.

She immediately detected his lustful stare and stepped forward in shameless confidence. Now that the danger had passed, she needed to make a lasting impression. The male was obviously vulnerable.

"I can assure you we weren't bothered by your inquiry," she purred. "And as I said before, we will notify your friends that you're looking for them." She untied her glossy red hair and let it fall around her pulled-back shoulders. Although she was clothed in sweats, any man could see that great beauty existed beneath. She casually lifted a little of her sweatshirt to reveal a tanned, toned stomach. She scratched at an invented itch and lowered her clothes with a seductive smile.

"Well, thank you for your concern. We better be on our way." The female's jealous voice put the male's eyes back in their place. She gave his hand a hard tug, and he followed her obediently up the hill.

Avangeline waited until the guests were out of sight before she turned to me and beamed. "Are you sure you don't want to give us a chance, Tristan? I think we make a cute couple." She took a step closer and smoothed back my hair that covered my eyes.

I studied her face that begged for my affection and gently lowered her hand. She had a lot to learn about people. She didn't understand the complexity of my broken relationship, neither did she want to. The animal in her nature didn't have time for compassion or the understanding of such matters. All she knew were her instincts. The challenge wasn't for a mermaid to acquire legs, but to acquire a heart. I looked past her face to the water that spread across the horizon. My eyes focused on a small moving object. Gwendolyn's head could be seen bobbing up and down in an ocean that seemed so very vast.

Avangeline cleared her throat to divert my attention. "I can't wait to see this club you've spoken of. And your apartment? Are you sure I can stay there until I find a place of my own?"

I averted my eyes from the tragedy at sea and turned toward the dimly lit parking lot. My black sports car glowed under a streetlamp that was shared with a lone white truck—presumably Ryan's. "Yes," I answered as I started for the hill. "You can stay with me as long as you need to. And I'll show you La Mer first thing tomorrow. Come on, it's getting late. The parking lot is up this way."

As I silently led her through the night, I ignored the many 'oohs' and 'aahs' she squealed as she explored new things. The lifeguard station's wooden structure, a fire pit with ashen logs, thorny bushes that hedged in the street, pavement—all were exciting discoveries to a mermaid who was held prisoner by the ocean. She stopped before getting into my car and ran her hand down the length of the passenger's side window.

"Glass . . . look how shiny it is. It's so smooth. It's so . . ." She stopped mid-sentence and stood rigid. Something caught her eye that she was destined to fall in love with—her reflection. Her gray eyes widened with sheer adoration as she inspected every inch of her face. She pursed her already full lips and grabbed two fistfuls of her hair, piling it high atop her head. She pushed out her chest to get a good look at her physique and cocked her head to one side. "I'm beautiful, aren't I? I've seen glimpses of myself in the metal of ships, but I've never seen it so clear." She examined herself one last time before sliding into my seat with a sigh. "I'm absolutely gorgeous."

"Well, of course you're gorgeous," I grunted, suddenly annoyed with her pride. I slammed her door and got in. "What did you expect to look like? You're designed to attract humans."

"Yes, I suppose you're right. But these humans won't know what hit them. They'll be begging for mercy when they see me. Hey! That feels strange when your car moves like that."

The blood in my veins burned with wrath as I made my way down GlenPoint Strip. Avangeline's voice was like a dripping faucet. The exclamations of wonder that came in a steady stream could not be turned off. Everything was shiny. Everything was flashing. Everything was new. She learned about her new world from the comfortability of my leathered seat while Gwendolyn most likely was suffocating above water. The cruel comparison of the two lives could not be overlooked. One relished the delicacies of the night, while the other would be lucky if they made it through.

"And green must mean go. Is that why your car moves? Marcus? Are you listening to me? *Did you hear anything I just said?*"

I gripped my steering wheel so hard my knuckles turned white. It was all I needed to lose total control. I parked my car at La Mer and turned off the ignition. I turned my body in her direction so I could get a good look at her face.

"Avangeline, let's just get something straight. Don't ever use common influence with me again. My thoughts are private, and I don't want you in them. And I'm not interested in having a relationship with you. Ever! What you pretended we were on the shore with Gwendolyn's friends will never happen. Don't get the wrong idea. I'm letting you stay with me so you can find a place to live. I don't want to be involved with you romantically. Understood?"

Her face contorted like she had sucked on a lemon. She opened her mouth to say something and then closed it.

She knew better than to abuse me with her words. She had nowhere to live, and she knew it. She drew in her breath with a hiss.

"Do you think you're the only man I'm going to be interested in? I'm sorry, but you're not that important. You may be good-looking, but not by your own merits. We're designed that way to attract humans, remember?" She found her face in my side mirror and studied it. "I'm sure there are plenty of attractive men who were born that way out of nature. And I know all of them will worship me. I really have no use for your flatteries." She looked up from her reflection and chuckled. "And thank you for allowing me to live with you for a time. Your apartment looks . . . uh . . . nice."

I got out of the car and surveyed the crumbling brick building she stared at. La Mer was a lavish club that lay hidden within the city. Its rich tapestries, exotic food, and energetic music set it apart from the typical fare. GlenPoint's newer architecture and tourist-attracted shopping malls drew the crowds, but La Mer had its place. Those who didn't judge its outward appearance were rewarded with its offerings.

"We have to enter through the back of the club to get to my apartment. There's a staircase that will take us to the top. And, hey, try not to talk to anyone. They're working for me right now." I gave the parking lot a quick glance and noticed the abnormal amount of cars that were still left.

"Oh! I get to meet humans?"

I gave her a scowl and opened the back door.

"Surprise!" The room cheered.

My eyes adjusted to the dim lights and found a handful of workers clapping in celebration. Some wore aprons and were finishing their shifts, while others were dressed in street clothes and came for the occasion. The night's shift supervisor stepped forward with a smile. "I read an announcement in GlenPoint's newspaper that said La Mer has been voted the best restaurant in the city. We thought we would surprise you with a little something to celebrate. It's not much, but . . ." She handed me a bottle of champagne and pointed to a nearby table with a cake. "Well, congratulations! We're really happy for you."

My face flushed hot with unexpected emotion. I never received a gift before. The unforeseen gesture of kindness not only renewed my faith in humanity, but it nearly brought me to tears. I pulled at my collar and coughed. "Wow. Thank you, everyone." I looked to the floor and struggled to find the right words. "I didn't know our restaurant was doing so well. I have to say it's because of all your hard work. It's really great to have you all on my team. Thank you for getting us here. It really means a lot."

I glanced around at the half-circle of coworkers and frowned. No one appeared to have listened to a single word I said. No one moved. No one even looked in my direction. All eyes were fixed on the glorious woman that demanded for their attention. Even the dishwasher in the kitchen crossed to the back of the room to gawk. I shook my head and continued, "Thank you for your kindness. It really was unexpected. Now, if you all will excuse me, I think I'm going to turn in."

"Well, don't turn in just yet, boss," the cook interjected in an unusual show of boldness. He looked to Avangeline and blushed. "I'm sure you and your friend are hungry from the long night. Can I make you both something to eat?"

"I'm not hungry, Lance," I grunted, ignoring his dejected expression. "I'm tired. I appreciate your offer. But, no. It's getting late." I turned to Avangeline, who stood posed at my side. For the first time since we entered the building, I observed her baseless seduction. It didn't take common influence to see she had worked the whole room in her direction. I gave her arm a nudge to reel her in.

She looked at us startled as if she was caught doing something wrong. "Hungry? Yes, of course I'm hungry. Starving, in fact. Can you make me something from the ocean? Maybe some fish, perhaps?" She batted her fringed eyelashes that made Lance turn a deep shade of purple. He turned on his heel and sprinted to the kitchen.

I waited until the flustered cook was out of sight before I gave a hearty laugh. "It sure doesn't take much for you to get that guy going, does it? At this rate, he'll be feeding you dinner by hand." I took a seat at the table with the cake and sighed. "Well, I guess this means we're staying. Just don't take too long to eat. I want to get some rest." The delay was an inconvenience, but it prevented me from having to provide Avangeline with dinner. I reached for the bottle of champagne and looked down at the label.

"You're not doing me any favors by staying here," she hissed, smiling at a nearby busboy. He quickly picked up his washbasin and moved closer. "I don't need you to watch over me. I can take care of myself."

"Yes, I'm sure you can. But I don't trust you. Besides, I have to show you my apartment. Remember?"

She shrugged in agreement and continued to flirt. Together we sat in silence as she and the workers danced a mental tango of lust. A server crossed from the corner of the room to fold napkins.

"You don't have to try too hard with them, you know." I looked up as Lance approached our table. He set down a steaming plate of crab legs and bowed. Avangeline's groan of pleasure made him nearly topple over a chair. "They're drawn to your looks, but don't be fooled. They won't want to get to know you or have a meaningful relationship. It's all superficial. Humans can't get past the outward appearance." I looked down at the bottle I was still holding and closed my eyes with sadness.

"Can I open that for you, sir?" Lance asked, returning to our table. He set down two fluted glasses and a corkscrew. "Is your guest twenty-one?"

I looked to Avangeline, who nodded at his question. "Yes, we're both old enough to drink. But I never—." I paused and pondered my next move. I never had a sip of alcohol in my life. There was nothing about the beverage that attracted me. To my observation, those who lingered long at the glass became humbled by its contents. I saw people enter my club with grace and dignity, only to stumble out the door in dishonor and shame. It was a beverage given to those who would rather relinquish their power. It was a beverage given to those who would rather forget who they were. I flinched at the thought of Gwendolyn suffocating above water.

"Sure, Lance," I said, holding up my glass. "I guess a little drink won't hurt."

Chapter Three

I opened my eyes in total darkness. The thick object that squeezed around my throat tightened.

"Speak your name before I kill you!" a shrill voice commanded within my mind.

My body thrashed violently in an unexpected rush of adrenaline. I grasped the slippery muscle that wrapped around my neck and dug my nails deep into its flesh. Its grip loosened, and a woman's scream exploded in my head. I pushed away the slithering object that groped for my arms and surged toward the surface. Her hand seized me by my wrist and pulled me back down under the water.

"Speak! Speak, you idiot! Speak!"

I scrambled to pry her fingers off my arm, but they held on even tighter. My burning lungs squeezed within my chest.

"Speak!"

I tugged from her grip and kicked my tail, but she wouldn't let go. The pulse in my head thundered with terror.

"Say your name! What's your name?"

A crushing pressure burst within my ribcage. Excruciating pain radiated down my arm, and my jaw locked tight.

"Why can't you talk? Speak! What's the matter with you?!"

The shadows of my vision faded to black. The person who held my wrist shook my arm. She cried out in frustration and shook my arm again.

"Take a breath! Breathe! Breathe, you lily-livered scum! You're killing yourself!"

My desire to swim to the surface slowly vanished. The muscles in my body relaxed, and I stopped flapping my tail. I released the hand that held my wrist and succumbed to the darkness that enveloped me.

"Breathe!"

I floated on a gentle-moving current and gave up my struggle. The voice that yelled obscenities in my head dwindled to silence. The pain that spread across my chest ceased. The fight I waged within my body and spirit was surrendered to the will of the enemy.

I saw my father.

He slowly entered my bedroom and looked down to the floor. There I lay, exposed in my new form, desperate to hide from his view. He knelt to one knee and gently tilted my chin. His loving eyes held mine, and he smiled.

The woman's hand that held my wrist pulled hard.

I opened my mouth to scream and sucked in two lungs full of water. The crisp, sparkling liquid converted into air and nourished my thirsty bloodstream.

I breathed.

I breathed deep. The breath I drew was the cleanest air from the tallest mountain. My body strengthened as I drank it in. I drank it in over and over. I couldn't get enough.

"What's your name?"

I opened my eyes in horror.

With one strong kick of my tail, I broke free from the person that held me captive and shot straight to the top.

I burst through the water with a gargled cry and swam in sheer panic toward the shore. The splash of breaking water sounded from behind me, followed by the sloshing of movement. My pursuer was fast as she quickly closed in. She grasped me by the edge of my fin and pulled me to herself.

"Wait! What's your name? Why were you trying to kill yourself?" She gave a deep chuckle and released my tail, propelling me forward.

I halted in my desperate attempt to flee and spun around to face the person who tormented me. I burst into a spasm of coughs and recoiled.

A mermaid of magnificent splendor swam before me.

Her smooth black skin was as rich as onyx, glittering with droplets of water that reflected light from a moonlit sky. Silky black hair fell past her shoulders in ringlets, framing a perfectly sculpted body. Her full lips frowned as she waited for my response.

"You hurt my tail," she whined, looking to her waist. "You know, when you scratched me to get away? I hope it doesn't leave a scar." She rose out of the water high enough to expose her belly and the silvery conversion to scale. She inspected a small mark by the light of the moon and slowly lowered back in. "It will definitely leave a scar." She removed a piece of seaweed from her breast and looked up with a smirk. "What's the matter with you? Why can't you talk? Are you mute or something?"

"I . . . I . . . can talk."

"Well, I can see that now. But why didn't you answer me when I asked for your name? And why were you trying to commit suicide? I was going to kill you for trespassing in my territory, but . . ." Her voice trailed, and her gray eyes searched mine. Her pupils widened, and she looked deep within my heart. *"What's wrong with you?"* she questioned, probing within my mind.

"I wasn't trying to kill myself," I muttered, turning away from her stare. "I was trying to breathe. I couldn't get enough air even though I . . . I mean—" I puffed and grimaced as the familiar tightness in my lungs began to take hold. "I don't know how to breathe underwater. I'm used to breathing air."

"I'm not understanding what you're trying to say. You're a mermaid, right? But you don't know how to breathe? Do you mistake me for being simple-minded? Surely you know how to—" Her eyes widened, and she gasped. "What are you?"

"I'm not a mermaid," I said between sputters. "I just became one tonight. I watched as my fiancé got murdered, and I didn't do anything about it. My new body is my punishment, I guess."

She squealed so high I cringed. She grasped me with both hands and swung them back and forth. "Yes! Of course! It's the traitor's curse. That explains why our common influence is so limited. You haven't fully accepted the ocean yet. My father told me all about the cursed. He said you're very useful for giving us information. Can you teach me about humans? I can teach you about entrapping one." She released my hands with another shriek and bobbed up and down. "Oh! I can't believe I met a traitor. I hope we can become the closest of friends. My name is Sabrina, by the way."

I choked on the air that tickled my throat and gave a wobbly smile. The pendulum swung from murderer to best friend in less than ten minutes. I was nearly strangled by her tail, and I was embraced like a long lost friend. The stark change of heart was a little hard to believe.

"I'm Gwendolyn," I wheezed. "And I think I can't breathe."

"Of course you can't breathe, silly. Your bloodstream ran out of oxygen. You have a limited supply to function on the surface. You can slither up the shore to, you know, have a quick conversation with a cute guy. But after that, you begin to suffocate. You need to replenish your oxygen levels by breathing in the water. It's just the way things work."

"It may be the way things work," I choked between sputters. "But it's pretty frightening to perform. That's how humans drown."

"Well, you're not a human anymore, are you? Welcome to your new world. The ocean is where you will truly experience life. Allow me to take you to safer waters. I can help you take your first breath, too. Conscious that is, anyways." She giggled and grasped me by both hands. Her eyes held mine as she waited for me to comply.

I bit my lower lip and looked past her face to the shore. There was something about the moment that felt strangely off. It was as if I was at the crossroads, and I was about to choose the wrong direction. Her offer of companionship was shallow, and her obvious ulterior motive made me doubt it would ever become genuine, but an alliance with another mermaid was a gift I couldn't deny.

"Are you ready?" she asked, breaking through my thoughts.

I took another look at the shadowed expanse of sand and gave a halfway nod.

She flashed a mischievous grin, and we quickly lowered in. Her hand held mine tight as she led me farther and farther from the world I once knew. Shrouded silhouettes of sleeping fish drifted along our path as we made our way deep into the heart of the ocean. The water became cool and dark, and a crumbly seabed slowly came into view. Although I could barely see Sabrina's face, I could tell she was brimming with excitement.

"Okay, let's stop right here. Now just float. Let all the muscles in your body relax. You're going to take a deep breath through your mouth and let it out through your nose. When I count to three, I want you to breathe like you would on land. Just picture you're standing on the shore and there's nothing holding you back. Are you ready? Don't fight the desire, Gwendolyn, your body wants to do this. Ready?"

I winced from the burning in my chest and reached for Sabrina's other hand. Although I was able to hold my breath for the entirety of our swim, the physical exertion of traveling depleted all my remaining reserves. My lungs were sore and heavy, and I was tired. I wanted nothing more than to become one with the ocean that waited.

"It's now or never. Are you ready? One, two, three!" She gave my hands an encouraging squeeze, and I took in the deepest breath I could.

A kaleidoscope of color burst across my vision as the torrent of water entered my bloodstream. Everything became alive with my breath. Black water transformed to the deepest shade of sapphire. The mysterious seabed that hid within the shadows rippled with polyps of purple and orange. Bright pink sea anemones and black-and-white speckled limpets covered a craggy rock that jutted from its surface. I swam to get a closer look at its beauty and touched the shell of a tiny orange hermit crab. I pulled away my hand and blinked with disbelief.

I could taste his fear!

The bitter pith of grapefruit filled my mouth as he scurried to a crevasse and hid. My skin prickled with gooseflesh, and I shuddered with empowerment. I could taste emotion! I could savor Sabrina's honey-sweet happiness for finding a cursed friend, and the stale bread of laziness from a floating sea turtle in the distance. The more my body took in the ocean, the more my senses fine-tuned to perfection. I was a mermaid filled with power, and I was flawless in every way.

"Well? What do you think?" Sabrina asked, watching me take it all in. Her face became amused as I pointed to a parrotfish. *"Any changes from living on land?"*

I laughed at the obvious question and tickled his belly with my finger. *"Changes from living on land? Sabrina, are you kidding me? This is amazing! I can't believe I'm actually able to talk to you in my thoughts! And I can sense your emotion, too. It's like I can taste it. It's the weirdest thing I've ever experienced."*

"We call that common influence," she informed, turning abruptly from our conversation. She swam across the ocean's powdery floor and pulled me along using gentle control. She halted by a forest of dark green sea kelp, and I stopped. *"Do*

you feel that? That's me guiding you to where I want you to go. It's a nerve we share that's connected through our common influence. Our thoughts and control of movement are all interconnected. Watch for it in this school of fish." She waved her hand above her head and hundreds of silvery sardines darted out of the tangle of vegetation. They turned in unison like the wheels of a car and swam in the same direction. She watched the whirlpool of panicked prey before she reached in their midst and caught one. Hungrily, she tore off its head and devoured its flesh. *"It's a pretty useful sense to have when you're swimming amongst predators,"* she mumbled between mouthfuls. *"And I hear it's pretty useful to have on land, too."*

My stomach suddenly dropped as the tormented face of Marcus surfaced from the middle of nowhere. He tried to prove he was once a merman by using common influence. Although I was able to hear his voice in my head, I was unwilling to accept what he had to say. My reaction to his confession was foolish and indifferent. Had I heeded his warning of Ryan's infidelity in our relationship, I wouldn't have become a mermaid.

"Who's Marcus?"

"What?"

Sabrina's voice cut through my memories like a knife. The invasion of my privacy instantly flared my nerves. It was one thing to communicate through thought and emotion, but it was another to actually pry in and see them.

Her eyes narrowed at the change in my voice. *"Marcus. You thought of someone named Marcus. He has slicked black hair and slate gray eyes. A body sculpted by the gods. Gorgeous man, really. Was he once a merman?"*

I pushed her out of my head with such force that she flung back. My mouth immediately filled with the coppery taste of blood. I couldn't tell if it was her wrath, or if I bit my tongue.

"*He's no one important,*" I lied. I swam toward her and clenched my hands in tight fists. "*How are you able to see my thoughts? And why can't I see yours?*"

She stared at me in shock as if I punched her in the face. The fizz of carbonated water tickled my tongue.

"*I don't know. Maybe we're only able to see each other's thoughts in part. Maybe you can't see mine because you haven't mastered your senses yet. There's always someone who has more control than the other. For the moment, it appears as though I have more than you. That may change as you grow accustomed to your environment.*" Her forehead furrowed in a scowl. "*But why did you get so upset? I simply asked a question.*"

My face grew hot, and I looked the other way. I didn't know why I lost my temper. I wasn't someone who was quick to get mad, but her meddling in my thoughts struck an unforeseen chord. It was a violation of privacy. The reaction to push her away came as natural as breathing.

"*I'm very sorry I offended you, Sabrina. I'm not sure why I became so upset. I wouldn't have responded that way if I was a human.*"

The lines in her forehead softened, and she gave an understanding nod. "*I'm sure you became a true mermaid when you took your first conscious breath of water. I suppose there will be some minor adjustments to who you were on land.*" She swam to where I floated and snaked her arm around my shoulder. She chuckled when I stiffened and gave it a gentle squeeze.

"I'll forgive you for getting upset. After all, I just tried to kill you, remember? I guess we're both even now."

We chorused in laughter, and I thanked her for her understanding. Perhaps my assumption of Sabrina's friendship was wrong. If she was willing to give me her patience while I learned the ropes of being a mermaid, I was willing to give her my trust and cultivate a genuine relationship.

After a moment of exchanging heartfelt apologies, she suggested for me to follow her to safer waters, and we swam to an area that was thick with kelp. Everywhere I looked, fish slept within the folds of brown and green vegetation. I rubbed my eyes and blinked in overwhelming fatigue. The hellish events that demanded for a rush of adrenaline had finally taken their toll.

"So, where will we sleep tonight? Do you live in a sunken ship or something?" I asked, looking around for a shelter.

"A sunken ship?" She laughed and gestured for us to stop. *"Are you serious? That would be the last place I would reside. Humans are always exploring those sites. I don't sleep anywhere where I'll get caught."*

She grasped a fistful of kelp and tied the smooth leaves around her wrists. After ensuring the plant was firmly attached, she pulled the massive structure around her body and disappeared inside. Her silvery fish's tail poked out through the tangled bottom. *"I don't live anywhere in particular. As a mermaid, you always have to be one step ahead of the human. If I made myself a home, it would ultimately be discovered."* Her arms reached through the floating curtain in a tired stretch. *"This spot seems good enough to sleep tonight. The ocean's floor is at a safe distance from the shore, and the plants will hide us from predators. Just make sure you tie them around your wrists so you don't drift from its concealment."*

I swam to a lush spot at her side and tucked myself into the slippery pleats. Then, just as I saw Sabrina demonstrate, I tied the thick blades securely around my wrists and buried myself deep into the plant. The gentle sway of current lulled me into a trance.

"Sabrina?"

"Yes?"

"Will you be there when I wake up?"

"Yes, of course. When the waters brighten and the fish stir, the humans will come to the shore to gather. Maybe we can try to entrap one. I already have my eye on a promising prospect."

"Really?" I tried not to sound too disappointed. The thought of losing my new friend to a life on the shore brought an unexpected pang of sadness. *"Tell me about him."*

It took a while for Sabrina to respond. I wasn't sure if the delay was due to fatigue or carefully selected words.

"I haven't had a chance to talk to him yet. We made eye contact several times while he was surfing, but he was with another girl so he didn't approach me. I can tell he's very interested, though."

"Does he know you're a mermaid?"

"No. The tricky part is to stay below the water so people don't see your tail."

"What does he look like?"

"He's about my age. Maybe nineteen, or so. He always visits this same location. You know, lifeguard station twelve. He's pretty easy to spot since he changes his hair to so many different colors. Last I saw, he had red and blue braids."

I felt my face drain of color. She was interested in Ryan's best friend, Joey.

"Don't worry about finding someone, Gwendolyn. You will. Humans are always led by what they see. I don't know if you know this or not, but we're the most beautiful creatures that ever existed on earth. You will have no trouble entrapping a man. I can assure you of that."

I closed my eyes and tried to block the information she just shared. Her common influence hadn't detected my thoughts of Joey, and I wanted to keep it that way. I tried to think of anything else that would bring comfort to my troubled heart. I fumbled with memories of my past life on land and found no peace.

"Goodnight, Gwendolyn."

"Goodnight, Sabrina."

Chapter Four

I staggered through the doorway of my apartment and tripped on the mat in the entrance. The empty bottle of champagne fell from my grasp and shattered to the floor with a crash. I slipped on the remnant of alcohol that was spilled and toppled on the broken glass. A large shard cut through my pants and pierced the side of my leg.

"Oh, Marcus! Are you okay? You're not hurt, are you?" Avangeline stepped around my body and entered the dark living room. "Where's the lights in this place?" she asked, immediately abandoning her concern. She looked to me and then around herself as if she was unsure of where she was. "Why are your walls colored white? This is it? You actually live here?"

I attempted to stand with shaky legs, but my apartment took a hard spin. I fell to the littered floor and cut the palm of my hand. The sharp pain quickly subsided from the overwhelming presence of alcohol in my system. "This is where I live," I slurred, sweeping away some of the broken bottle with the back of my hand. "Why? Don't you like it? Because if you don't like it, then I don't like it." I burst into laughter at the sight of her disgusted expression.

She glared at me and crossed her arms across her chest. "Do you know you're lying in glass? Why did you drink that whole bottle of champagne tonight? I thought the stuff tasted disgusting. Besides, it's making you act like an idiot." She cleared away a piece of the bottle with her foot.

I looked up and gave her a lopsided grin.

"Are you sure you really live here?" she grunted, turning around to get another look at my living quarters. She walked to the hallway leading to my bedroom and stopped. "Your club is so beautiful—brightly colored walls and plush chairs. But here . . . well, I thought you would've put some of that effort in your own home." She ran her hand along a crack in the wall and shook her head.

Using all the strength I had left, I held onto the doorway and pulled myself to a wobbly stand. With one hand I pushed the front door closed, and with the other I reached for the light switch and missed. "Well, I'm sorry to have disappointed you. I don't live in some magic castle, if that's what you're expecting. But, hey, we can pretend we live in one. Why don't you call me King Marcus? That sounds good, doesn't it? I'll call you Queen Avangeline, if you'd like."

"Where am I supposed to sleep tonight?" she inquired, ignoring my jest. She disappeared into my bedroom and gasped. "There's clothes all over the floor! And only one bed?" She returned to the living room and released her breath loudly.

"Humans sleep in beds, right? They need a place to lie down when they rest. How is this going to work? Surely you won't make me sleep on that." She pointed to the loveseat by the window and sat in it.

"Listen," I uttered, releasing the wall with a sway. I stumbled into the living room and steadied myself against the window's drawn curtains. "Don't freak out. Humans sleep in beds, and you can sleep in mine. I'll sleep on the chair until we figure it all out. Just stop worrying about everything."

I fumbled for the curtain's string and pulled it. She exhaled as they parted, and a panoramic view of GlenPoint Strip was suddenly revealed. The twinkling lights of skyscrapers and traffic bathed her skin in a golden glow. Her wide, almond-shaped eyes took in every detail. She giggled as an automatic billboard changed from one picture to the next.

"What a beautiful view," I breathed, blinking to focus my eyes.

"Yes, it is. There's so much I couldn't see from the ocean. I grew tired of the same old sand dunes and lifeguard stations. Not to mention the annoying seagulls that would fly—"

"I wasn't talking about the city," I corrected.

"What?"

"I'm not talking about the city." I took a step closer.

She looked at me in confusion. "What are you talking about?"

I sank to my knees and fell in a mesmerized stare. My eyes burned, and I blinked. "I'm talking about you."

Her expression vacillated from perplexed to shock. "What?"

The room whirled beneath me in a dizzying spin, but her silhouette in the chair remained motionless. I felt for the floor and steadied myself with the palms of my hands. "You look beautiful tonight, Avangeline. I don't know why I haven't noticed this before, but when the light hits your face like that you look like an angel."

There was a brief pause as she gauged her situation. Her eyes raked mine for answers. "Are you serious?"

"Your eyes are so captivating. And your lips . . . they're so . . . so . . ." I licked my own for moisture and swallowed. "I can't stop looking at you." I inched myself closer to where she sat until I was kneeling at her feet.

She sat up tall in her chair. "But didn't you just say you didn't want to be involved in a romantic relationship?"

"Did I say that? Well, maybe I changed my mind. I probably wasn't thinking straight or something." I fumbled with the buttons of my collared shirt and took it off. My perspiration-soaked tank top cooled against my hot skin. I reached above my head and flexed in a tired stretch.

"I don't understand, Marcus." She paused to stare at my chest. "You've never been attracted to me before."

I crumpled my shirt into a tight ball and threw it across the room. The last hour at La Mer made me feel a lot of things I haven't felt before. The releasing of power brought a state of madness and shame. Every time my past threatened to resurface, I poured myself another glass. Before I knew it, I was a blubbering fool saying things I usually wouldn't say and doing things I usually wouldn't do. If it wasn't enough that Avangeline saw me in an abnormally giddy state, my whole staff saw me lose total control. I was a man who was regarded for his self-respect and authority. I was someone who governed his state of affairs with a permanent, unwavering scowl—and not because I was indifferent to human interaction, but because I chose not to become involved with those who would threaten my character. I wouldn't so much as smirk at the catty banter the servers engaged in during their shifts. And, yet, in one single night, I had become the topic of their future whispers. Everyone saw I was at the mercy of the busboy who helped me to the restroom. I was certain everyone snickered as I stumbled out the door. The disgrace would haunt me for weeks to come. It was enough to possibly trash my reputation.

"I don't know what I feel for you," I declared, becoming slightly annoyed. "But what difference does it make? All I know is that you're beautiful."

Her eyes narrowed, and she smiled. She reached forward and smoothed back my hair that fell before my brow. For the first time in our relationship, I allowed for her to touch me in affection. Her face lit with astonishment.

"This night is different, Avangeline. I've played the fool, and you're the one to benefit. You have me in the palm of your hand." I spread my hands across her lap and waited for her to grasp them. She looked down and gasped.

"Marcus, look! Your hand is bleeding. Don't you feel that?"

"I don't feel anything," I whispered, wiping it on the side of my pants. I reached for the back of her head and pulled her face toward mine. Her hair unraveled from its bun and fell around my shoulders. The cascade of red waves smelled heavily of salt, warm spices, and musk. I buried my nose in the side of her neck and took in a deep breath. "I don't feel anything but desire for you."

Within that moment of breathing her in, I knew I was making a grave mistake. The morning would dawn and the alcohol would fade, and my eyes would ultimately be opened. She would be my greatest regret.

Her body froze as if in fear. I pulled my head away from her hair and tried to focus on her face. Her eyes were dilated and on the verge of using common influence.

All at once, she lunged forward and pressed her mouth hard against mine in a kiss. Actions suspended in time as I lay in the arms of my seductress. Her lips were soft and sweet. They hungrily fed for mine. She caressed the length of my back while I ran my hands through her hair. I grasped a fistful of her curls and pulled her to myself.

I drank her in.

I drank in the putrefying dredges of her wicked soul. I drank in her lust—the selfish, cheap kind of lust that only wants one thing. I drank in her greed—the unquenchable desire that would kill a man for gain. I drank in her pride— the all-consuming narcissism that sought to rule the world. All at once, her lips that were once smooth and syrupy became like vinegar on my mouth. A burning liquid bubbled at the back of my throat, and my stomach twisted in knots. I pulled myself away from her embrace and covered my mouth with my hand. An unfamiliar sensation made my whole body feel sick.

"What is it?" she whispered. Her glazed eyes opened for a mere second before closing again. Desire kept her from seeing my plight. She pulled my hand away from my mouth and kissed me with unbridled passion.

An image of my victim, Emma, flashed within my mind. She smiled and tucked a long strand of hair behind her ear.

Her cheeks flushed pink as I mentioned my need for a kiss. She closed her eyes and puckered.

The acidic liquid surfaced on my tongue, and my stomach squeezed with cramps. I pulled away from Avangeline's face and stood to my feet in haste.

"What's wrong with you?" she asked. She rose from the chair and put her hands on her hips. Her once adoring eyes had become daggers.

I hugged my middle with trembling arms and tried to calm my nerves. My whole body shook from a cold sweat that appeared out of the middle of nowhere. "I don't know. I feel sick."

"Sick? What do you mean you feel sick?"

"I've seen it happen to customers who drink too much alcohol. They vomit."

"Vomit? What's vomit?"

Before I could answer her question, the contents of my stomach burst onto the floor. She screamed in horror and backed away.

"Eww! You got it on me! You got it on my feet! What is it?!"

I turned in the direction of the bathroom and took off in a wobbly run. I barely made it to the kitchen's floor before I threw up again.

"Oh, that's disgusting! How do I get it off me? It stinks!"

The muscles in my stomach burned from exertion as I continued to purge the alcohol. I gasped wildly for air and bent at my waist in pain. I vomited again and again. I threw up so many times I thought I would die. I looked up with teary eyes and cried out in sheer anguish. The door of the bathroom was at the end of the hallway, but it seemed like it was an eternity away.

"Can't you stop doing that? Come on! It's covered all over the floor."

Sweat rolled down the length of my back, and my legs buckled from fatigue. I gripped the kitchen counter for support and uttered a feeble prayer for help. Another wave of nausea hit, and I bent at my knees and lurched.

Avangeline entered the room from behind me and choked with a sound of disgust. "Ugh! How will this ever get cleaned up? Can't you stop doing that, Marcus? Marcus!"

My stomach knotted into a tight ball, and I hacked with a gargled cry. Although I wasn't finished purging, my illness transitioned to a dry heave. The more my body went through the motions, the more I felt closer to normal. After a few fruitless attempts of doing nothing more than gagging, I slowly lifted to a shaky stand and wiped my mouth with my hand. The nausea that crippled me from crossing the room had subsided to a manageable unease. I spit the remnant of vomit in my mouth and breathed a sigh of relief.

Avangeline clucked her tongue in disapproval. "Does that mean you're finished? I sure hope it does. I don't know how you're ever going to clean all of this up, but you need to do it fast. It smells putrid. There's no way—"

"Hey, Avangeline? Shut up."

"What?"

She stiffened in the doorway as my words obviously offended her. I didn't care. Her presence in my home was already beginning to weigh. I was such a fool to suggest for her to stay with me. I was such a fool to allow for her to touch my mouth. The memory of her vinegary lips pressed against mine made my stomach threaten to rebel.

I took in a few nauseated breaths and motioned for her to move out of the way. After gathering myself as best as I could, I pushed past her presence that barricaded the doorway and ran to the bathroom.

Chapter Five

I awoke just in time for breakfast. My stomach growled at the thought of hot pancakes drenched in maple syrup. I pulled back my covers with a groggy yawn and swung my legs over my bed. There was something about the way the floor felt beneath my feet that made me pause for thought. I looked down at the blur of carpet and clothes and focused on my pink painted toenails. Nothing about my feet seemed out of the ordinary. I wiggled my toes to inspect each one and slowly took a stand. Something wasn't right.

"Gwendolyn!" My mother's voice sounded eager.

I dismissed the reservations I had for the moment and turned to cross the room. The movement of my walking was effortless and fluid, floating almost, as I made my way to my dresser. I stopped in front of my full-length mirror and stared at my reflection. It was me that stood in the glass, but a perfect me. My frizzy blonde hair that was always so stubborn in the mornings hung in smooth waves. Blemishes on my face had vanished, and my lips were pink and full.

"Gwendolyn! Wake up!"

There was one change that didn't make sense. I leaned forward and squinted to get a better look at my eyes. They had changed color. Beneath the long fringe of curled eyelashes, two metal gray eyes opened wide in shock.

"Gwendolyn, wake up! It's time to entrap a human!"

Turquoise.

All I saw was turquoise. For a moment, I thought I was still dreaming. I attempted to pull up from my bed, but I couldn't move my arms. Long shafts of seaweed bound my wrists in place. Someone nudged me from behind, and I snapped them off to turn.

"Gwendolyn? Are you awake? It's time to get up. It's time to entrap a human."

"Huh? Okay." I blinked in confusion. A creature seen only in fairytales appeared out of the forestry of kelp. Her silver fish's tail fanned slowly in the breaking sun, creating clouds of golden bubbles that covered us both in sparkle. Ringlets of black hair floated past her ebony shoulders, enveloping a perfectly sculpted torso and two exposed breasts. She gave my arm a playful nudge and laughed when I pulled away.

"I heard you mumbling in your sleep. Were you dreaming?"

I looked down at the tail that extended from my waist and covered my face with my hands. It was real. All of it. The murder. The transformation. The future entrapment for my freedom. I've never woken from a dream to discover my reality was a nightmare.

"I almost used common influence to see what you were dreaming about. But I didn't want to pry. You got so angry when I read your thoughts yesterday."

I wanted to go back to sleep. I wanted to crawl back into bed and wake up to the smell of pancakes. If only it was my mother waking me up and not Sabrina. My heart broke at the thought of my parents discovering my absence from the night.

"Well, are you ready to entrap a human? It may take a few encounters, but you never know. You may get lucky." She pulled a long tendril of seaweed out from my hair and twirled it around her finger.

I looked up at the mermaid that knew no other way and gave a nod of resolve. Strength. At that moment, I needed to conjure strength. I needed to dig deep within myself and find the confidence it took to survive in a world of bloodshed. The grief of my past was legitimate, and perhaps I would never see my parents again, but those feelings were a hindrance that would prevent me from becoming human. I needed to suppress my anguish so deep that not even Sabrina knew it existed—even if I had to fake it at first.

"I can't wait to entrap a human! I've thought about it all night, actually. You know, what I'm going to say and how I'm going to say it. I guess I can use my relationships with old boyfriends to help me know how to act." I took in a deep breath of water and held it. A little embellishment about my experience on land wouldn't hurt anybody. It would keep Sabrina interested and possibly put me in control.

Her wide eyes scanned mine rapidly. *"Boyfriends? Really? Can you tell me about them? I've always wanted to know more about human relationships."*

I let the suspense build for a moment and swam out from our shelter of foliage. The pleats of vegetation parted to an ocean that was alive with movement. Sunlight bathed a pod of bottlenose dolphins that spun and twirled in the distance. Countless schools of tiny fish conjured into large groups of twinkling orbs. A shadow was cast from a manta ray above, and they broke apart and scattered. Sabrina followed close behind as I swam along the ocean's floor.

"What do you want to know?" I asked, dodging a trailing tentacle of a jellyfish.

She paused for a moment and stammered. *"Well, I don't know . . . there's so much to learn. What can you tell me about love?"*

"Love? Well there's all different kinds of love. There's the love that we have for things. Like eating a cold piece of pizza, wearing fleece pajamas, or reading a good book. We say we love those things, but that's not the same love we share for people."

"Pizza?"

"It's baked dough with tomato sauce and cheese. Sometimes we put toppings on it like pepperoni and olives. Oh, never mind." I stopped my mindless swimming to watch a group of crabs scurry across a rock. My stomach growled at the thought of food. *"There's the love we have for friends. My best friend Emma was so close she could probably read my mind. Not literally of course, but we could finish each other's sentences. We did everything together."* I turned my head and closed off the thoughts of her death as Marcus's victim. The painful recollection would elicit questions I didn't want to answer. My attention fled from Sabrina's face and focused on the crustaceans. *"And then there's the love a man shares with a woman."*

"I want to know more about that love! Tell me about it."

"Well, true love is when you meet the right person and you find you can't live without them. It's a lot like the love for a friend, only there's usually a mutual attraction. It isn't all about looks though—so much as who they are. Anything else is just lust."

"Lust?"

"A fleeting emotion. It's centered on attraction. It feels real for the moment, but when someone prettier comes along the relationship falls apart." My eyes narrowed on the bitter memory of Ryan caressing Avangeline on the shore. She was a mermaid perfect in appearance, and I was a human riddled with flaws. The choice for him to cheat on me was a no-brainer. He threw away our relationship built on experiences and trust to feed the lust of his flesh. Perhaps his death as Avangeline's victim couldn't have been prevented. Perhaps he received what he deserved.

A crab scuttled close to my hand, and I reached for its legs and grabbed it. I tore apart the knobby shell and slurped out the greenish contents.

"You just used common influence! You just read my thoughts!" Sabrina cried.

"What?" I looked down at my empty hand and to Sabrina in confusion. I never grabbed a crab. I never tore apart its shell or ate its meat. The moment happened so fast that I didn't recognize it as her thoughts. *"Gosh, I'm sorry. I didn't know I was using common influence. Why did it just happen?"*

She smiled and reached deep into the rock's crevasse. She retrieved a writhing lobster and pulled off several legs with one yank. *"I don't know. Maybe you'll gain better control over your impulses with time?"* She popped the appendages into her mouth and tore off the remaining. *"At least you can see my thoughts now. That's a major part of our communication. It looks like you're becoming more like a mermaid and less like yourself. And that's a good thing."* She frowned and pointed to a crab that crawled within my reach. *"Are you going to eat that?"*

I looked down at the creature, who waved his claws wildly, and considered his unfortunate plight. He reeked of fear. The bitter taste of aspirin permeated my mouth as he tried his best to scurry away. He was the prey. I was the predator. I was hungry. He was food. Nature dictated that he should give his life for my need.

Without giving it a second thought, I seized him from behind and placed my thumbs on the underside of his shell. I felt for the weakest part in his center and pressed as hard as I could. He popped open like an egg on the edge of a bowl. I pressed my mouth to the broken mess and devoured the gelatinous insides. The earthy taste was different from the cooked crab I ate on land, but it was delicious, satisfying, and unexpectedly addictive. After thoroughly enjoying my catch, I reached for another and broke it in half. The fear made the meat taste even more savory.

"Wow! For never being a mermaid before, you sure know how to eat like one."

I wiped my mouth with the back of my hand and looked down at the pile of carnage on the sand. A total of eight crabs were eaten. My sudden callousness to death took me by surprise. I was more of a catch-and-release type of person. I never harmed an animal in my life. And it wasn't the hunger that fueled my violent rampage so much as my desire. After a while, I enjoyed killing them.

"Well, are you ready to entrap a human?" she asked.
"Yes."

We broke through the surface into the crisp, clear morning. The sun shone brightly over our heads and I squinted, feeling almost blinded by the rays. A strong breeze picked up, and a thin wisp of cloud lessened the glare.

"Don't worry about your eyes, Gwendolyn. They won't stay blurry for long. It takes a minute or two for things to adjust."

I shielded them with my hand and looked around at the span of cobalt blue. The world at our breast glittered and shined like a horizon of stained-glass windows that stretched as far as the eye could see. Several seabirds squawked in the distance, and I turned toward the shoreline to see them fly away. It felt odd being on the opposite side of land. Although we had traveled quite a ways from humanity, I could still see the lifeguard station with the large painted twelve. The day was early enough that the parking lot had no cars. All that remained was Ryan's truck.

"So, this is my territory," Sabrina announced, spreading her hands. "From the lifeguard station there, to that cluster of rocks over there, I've chosen this location to be my living space. It's mine. All mine. No one can come into my territory, and we can never leave."

"Why?"

"Because mermaids don't live together. We choose to live alone because we don't want to share our victims with each other. Another mermaid means more competition. Alliances can happen, obviously, but they're incredibly rare. That's why so few mermaids exist today. Relationships never get a chance to form."

I thought about Marcus and Avangeline's agreement to help each other succeed in becoming human. He broke apart my relationship with Ryan so she could entrap him.

"There was a couple who lived here once," she disclosed, almost as if she read my thoughts. "I stayed at a distance and waited until I no longer felt their presence. The male was released a while ago, and the female disappeared last night."

I kept my face expressionless.

"I was so excited to take over this location because it's prime for entrapping. There's always people coming to this part of the beach. I don't know why. It must have something to do with the tide pools, or something."

As if on cue, a van drove down the hill and turned into the parking lot. I looked to Sabrina for direction, and she motioned for me to wait.

"If another mermaid crosses our path, we kill them. No questions asked. If they have common influence, and they most certainly do, they know not to enter the waters of another mermaid. It's just that simple."

The doors of the vehicle opened and a large family exited.

"What if someone comes into your territory by mistake?"

"There are no mistakes."

The children ran excitedly to the shore while the adults unpacked their belongings. They spread a blanket on the sand and set up an umbrella.

"Have you ever killed a mermaid before?"

"Yes."

"How many?"

"Several."

I turned away from the frolicking youth to catch a glimpse of her expression. Her large gray eyes were pinned on the shore. Her jaw was clenched so tight a vein bulged down the side of her neck. She didn't need to explain her actions because there was nothing left to say. She was a soulless murderer and would be expected to do no less.

"Let's wait and see if anyone else shows up. It may take a few minutes. It may take all day. We just need to be patient. Just don't forget to breathe."

We stayed in the same location and watched as the family enjoyed their Saturday morning at the beach. We watched as they played in the water and ate a picnic lunch. We watched as they built sand castles and collected shells. We watched as they laid on towels and sunbathed. We observed the activity of lifeguard station twelve for what felt like an eternity. A few couples appeared for a romantic afternoon and cuddled. An old man dug with a shovel and filled a pail. There were two single females with dogs on leashes and a police car that circled the parking lot. A vendor selling ice cream from a street cart appeared for a moment and left. No one of interest presented themselves as contenders. The sky changed its color from pale blue to blush, marking the failed attempt of our first day.

Sabrina turned to me and sighed. "Well, I guess that's it. No luck for today."

"Yeah, no luck," I mumbled, noticing the police car again. It slowly entered the parking lot and stopped beside Ryan's truck.

"You know, you never told me about one type of love," Sabrina said, turning to leave.

"Which love is that?"

A policeman got out of his car and peered into Ryan's window.

"The love of a family."

"The love of a family?" I cocked my head to one side and looked at her with surprise. It seemed odd she would be interested in something so chaste.

She nodded with certainty. "Yes, that love. Do you remember the family that visited here earlier today? They did so many things together. They looked happy even though there was no physical attraction. I want to know how that works."

I turned my back on the shore and began to swim away. "The love of a family is different," I said, dismissing my thoughts about Ryan. "It isn't something you have to work for, like the love of a romantic relationship. It's something you're born into. It's an unconditional gift."

"An unconditional gift? Can you show it to me?"

"What?"

"Show me your memories."

"Show you my—what? Are you serious?" I stopped swimming and searched her face for any trace of sincerity. Her steel-hard eyes had softened, and her mouth was slightly downturned. A great deal of disparity could be seen within her expression. All strength and pride had completely melted away, and what remained within her demeanor made me want to cry. She was searching for something I never lacked. Perhaps it was something I took for granted. I blinked at the painful realization and nodded. "Yes. I can show you that love."

She reached for my hands and told me to remember my family. I closed my eyes and opened the doors I tried so hard to lock. At first, my attempt was difficult as I couldn't recollect how my parents looked. I probed and probed, but no image would appear. And then, at last, it came.

It was the Christmas when my father lost his job and took a janitorial position to provide presents. Tears streamed down his cheeks when I opened my new bike. I saw my mother help me when I was sick. She held back my hair so I could throw up in the toilet. I remembered the long nights when we played card games and traded marshmallows, and the outings to the movie theater eating popcorn. I saw my father teach me how to ride a bike and purposely fall to stop me from going down a hill. I came through the accident without a scratch, but he broke his arm.

A lump filled my throat, and I stifled a cry.

Sabrina gave my hands a gentle squeeze. "That's enough. You don't have to share anymore. Thank you for giving me a chance to feel that."

My eyes stung with tears, and I turned before they fell. "Don't you have a family?" I wiped my eyes before she noticed.

Her face flinched. She tilted her chin in an effort to appear strong, but her eyes told a different story. A dark shadow of pain crossed her appearance, and she slowly shook her head. "I guess I can show you something, too."

She gave a thin smile and instructed for me to concentrate on her memories. I closed my eyes and tried to quiet my heart that was racing. I didn't know what she was going to show me. It was difficult to stop my own thoughts from invading the moment. A seabird squawked loudly over our heads, and I squeezed my eyes tighter to think.

There was nothing to see in my mind. The shape of the vision was dark and without form. My tongue detected the acidity of vomit, perhaps from Sabrina's overwhelming anguish. A few minutes passed of watching and waiting, and the underwater world that looked so familiar slowly came into view.

He came.

A merman of great stature appeared within the backdrop of blue. His gruff voice commanded for me to swim faster. I tried my best to stay by his side, but my small tail couldn't keep up with his. He reached for my arm and gave it a painful tug. The image shifted and another mermaid emerged. He screamed obscenities that made her upset, and she turned around and fled. I cried and called her mommy, but she never came back. The scene changed again, and the water became red with blood. The merman laughed sadistically as he tore a sea lion apart for no apparent reason. I wept and begged for him to stop, but he ridiculed my weakness and told me I would never amount to anything.

"He's wrong!" I blurted out. I opened my eyes to stop the memories. "Your wicked father is wrong! You will amount to something! If this wasn't a vision, so help me, I would tear him apart myself!" The muscles in my forearms flexed from a sudden flood of wrath. I wouldn't think twice to commit murder on the spot.

Sabrina opened her eyes and looked down at my hands that were holding hers. It was hard to tell if she was crying or not. Her voice cracked, and she cleared her throat. "I'm okay. What happened in my past has helped me become a stronger fighter today. I don't love him, but I've forgiven what he's done."

I shook my head and let out a heavy sigh. It wasn't fair she was treated so harshly. She was abandoned by her mother and abused by her father. In my book, her past was completely unacceptable. Murderous villain, mermaid or not—everyone deserved a chance to be loved.

"I'm very sorry you had to experience those things." I gave her hands a squeeze. "I can't imagine what you went through. Your parents are monsters, and they don't deserve to have you as their daughter. But you know what? You are right about one thing. It doesn't matter what kind of a family you had because you have me now. You got that? I'm your family now."

She looked up at the change in my voice and smiled. A small tear trickled down her cheek before she gave me her back and sank beneath the surface.

Chapter Six

"*Gwendolyn! Hurry! I have something to show you.*"
I looked up from my breakfast of leatherback sea
turtle to find Sabrina flushed and out of breath.
Her wild eyes darted past me to the surface.

"*What is it? I'm not finished eating.*" I chewed my rubbery
mouthful and swallowed.

"*Come on,*" she insisted, reaching for my hand. She pulled
my wrist, and I dropped my meal. "*You can eat later. Follow
me before it's too late!*"

I slithered my hand out from her grasp and picked up
the scraped-out shell that fell to the sand. The urgency in her
voice was interesting, but not enough for me to leave my food.
Very little conjured excitement within the last six months of
living underwater. Our beach that bustled with youth and
excitement had changed since Ryan's and my disappearance. Convertibles and umbrellas were replaced with police

cars and yellow tape. Sabrina and I watched in despair as a crime scene unfolded that would take nearly three months to end. Still, after the investigation was over the foot traffic never returned to its original state. The once busy shores of lifeguard station twelve had all but become a ghost town. There was the occasional couple or picture-taking tourist, but no one of interest stayed for very long. Morning would turn into night. Night would turn into morning. Hopes would mount with the dawn of a new day, only to be dashed with the realization that life would never be the same. The routine was monotonous and predictably discouraging.

I shrugged my shoulders and reached deep into the slippery shell. A large chunk of meat dislodged with a satisfying pop.

Sabrina grabbed the carcass and tossed it. *"I'm serious! This really can't wait. The beach will be opening soon, and you'll miss out on your chance."*

"Miss out on what?" I picked up the shell again. *"You know no one comes here anymore. Besides, it won't take me very long to finish my food. What's so important that you can't wait?"*

Her eyebrow arched at my comment. She spun in a circle and flapped her tail to leave.

"Wait!" I called out. *"Where were you earlier today? I didn't see you when I woke up."* She looked over her shoulder and rolled her eyes with a groan. *"That's what I'm trying to show you!"*

I followed her at once and forgot my breakfast.

The morning was earlier than when we usually surfaced. Dark purple clouds covered a sun that was just beginning to rise. The parking lot was empty, but that was to be expected.

It was too early for the lifeguards to arrive. Even the great white albatross rested her weary wings as she dipped and bobbed on the surface. The only thing that changed from the day before was the unexpected presence of dark gray fishing boats that loomed like ghosts in the distance. One of them blew its horn, and I flinched.

Sabrina and I made eye contact before she pointed to the shore in command. We silently sank back into the water and swam in its direction. Distance stretched on for what felt like miles. Every time I expected for us to arrive, she turned around and motioned for me to continue. I finally called out for her to stop, and we quickly rose to the surface.

"What is it?" she asked out of breath. "We really need to hurry."

"Aren't we getting too close to the shore? I mean—we're almost to where the water breaks." My heart hammered at the thought of being seen.

She shook her head in frustration. "Yes, I know we're getting close. That's why we can't stop and talk. The last thing we need is for someone to see us and say something. We're going to surface near those rocks over there."

I squinted in the direction of her pointed finger and looked the other way. A lot happened at the horseshoe cluster of rocks. It was where Ryan was murdered. It was where I transformed. It was where Marcus saved me from drowning. I could still hear his screams of pain as he split his back on the rocks to shield mine.

"Be careful when you surface. Don't stiffen when the water meets the sand, or you're likely to get hurt. We don't need any broken bones when we get back home." She smiled at my reaction. "Stay flexible and let the waves guide you in. It's best if you let me go first."

She smoothed back her hair behind her ears and descended just enough for me to see her shoot out toward the coastline. I swam in her wake and watched for her to reappear on land. The water swelled and collected to white peaks before crashing to the shore and spilling across. The sparkling blanket of foam pulled back from the sand, and a larger wave raised higher than the first. It struck the earth with a thunderous boom, and a silvery fish's tail appeared with the water. Sabrina glided across the sand like a boat coming into shore, making the act of surfacing appear simple, effortless, and fluid. She lifted off the ground in a cobra-like stance and beckoned for me to join her.

I swallowed the lump that formed in my throat and dropped below the surface. The once passive current roared as I swam closer and closer to the breaking water. Wisps of frothy effervesce swirled above my head, and the ocean's pebbled floor slowly came into view. The space between the surface and the seabed grew more and more narrow. I extended my arms over my head and positioned myself for the mount. A wave pulled back with a sudden sway and punched me hard to the shore. My arms flailed wildly to gain control as I tumbled over the rock-studded sand. I spit out a mouthful of grit before Sabrina could arrive and notice.

"Not the most graceful surfacing," she teased, joining my side. She said something under her breath and offered me her hand. I lifted my torso with the thought of a stand and smoothed down my ruffled scales. "But not the worst surfacing either. Here's what I wanted to show you."

She slithered toward the craggy rocks and stopped at a small cave-like opening. For a few minutes she disappeared in its entrance and reappeared with two objects: a bright pink surfboard and the top of a black wetsuit. Her cheeks flushed dark with pride as she laid her newfound treasures on the sand. "So, what do you think? It's the perfect foil for our story of taking an afternoon swim."

I looked down at the unexpected offerings and back up at Sabrina in confusion. "I don't understand. Where did you get this stuff? How are we supposed to use a surfboard if we can't stand?"

"Oh, you of little imagination," she said with a sweep of her hand. She bent to the ground and wiped away the sand from the board. "We're not going to stand on it. We're going to drape over it. It adds plausibility to our presence in the water. It also gives me something in common with that gentleman with the red and blue braids. He used to come here to surf, you know."

"But—."

"Not to mention this thing will cover the scales on our waists and our exposed breasts that you say will cause too much attention. I don't know, I think it will fit . . ." She picked up the wetsuit top and stretched its rubbery material across her chest. "Yes. I think it will work just fine. What do you think?"

"I . . . I . . ."

"You know, you're acting incredibly rude just staring there with your mouth open. A simple 'thank you' will be enough."

"I'm not trying to be rude. I guess I'm just in shock. Yes, it will work." I felt myself begin to smile for the first time in months. The confidence of becoming human was slowly taking hold. "Yes! This will totally work. I can't wait to try them out. Oh, thank you so much, Sabrina. We can use them during the day and stash them here for safekeeping." I looked over my shoulder suddenly aware that we had been on the surface for too long. The clouds had almost completely burned off, and the highway that led to the beach's parking lot hummed with movement. "What if the owner comes back for them? What happens then?"

Sabrina smiled and prompted for me to put on the top. "Don't worry about her. She won't be back."

"What do you mean she won't be back?" I stretched the tight neckline over my head and bent my arms in an awkward position to put them through the sleeves. The act of getting dressed seemed almost foreign. "How can you be sure?"

"She's dead. I knocked her off her board and pulled her underwater. It was a pretty easy kill. She hardly fought back."

I felt my eyes widen. "What?"

"What's wrong? She deserved to die. She told me she snuck to the beach against her parents' wishes. She said something about it not being safe with the recent disappearances and all." The heartless mermaid shrugged her shoulders and looked toward the water. "Well, maybe she should've stayed home because she disappeared, too."

I bit my lower lip and focused on the pink surfboard with the black and white tropical flower pattern. Feelings of elation and guilt played tug of war within my mind. On one side, my dwindling shred of morality felt pity for the life that was lost—on the other, my animalistic nature cared only about myself. For the first time in months, I was given a hope that I could entrap a human without any fear of being seen as a mermaid. I was also wearing a wetsuit that someone just died in.

Sabrina turned from the ocean and smoothed my hair behind my ears. She pulled down the hem of my top and gave an approving nod. "You look beautiful in that thing. I can almost picture you as a human. Except for your tail that keeps flopping around so much."

We burst into laughter, and her face became serious. "Do you know when it's time to take a man's soul? When you know he loves you. When you're certain he'll give you his heart, you ask him for a kiss. I've heard that love tastes like salt."

"Salt?"

We turned toward the beach's parking lot and gasped. Several cars pulled into the lot.

Sabrina's eyes grew wide in terror. *"Get to the water!"* she screamed within my mind. Her tail whipped her body in a large semicircle, and she frantically dismounted from the rocks. *"I told you we needed to hurry! I begged, and begged, and begged for you to follow me. But, no! You had to be so stubborn. If only you would've listened sooner we wouldn't be here this late. You bloody fool!"* She slithered to the breaking water and dove in.

I grabbed the surfboard with trembling hands and followed her to the ocean. As I made my way to the water's edge, I took one look over my shoulder. A large group of males with surfboards were walking in my direction.

***

"So, why do you think you're qualified to work for La Mer?" I anticipated a genuine answer from the female who sat across the table, but once again I was sorely disappointed. Her mind quickly fashioned another lie.

"I've worked at a restaurant my family owned since I was young. I did all the jobs there, really. You know—serving, cleaning, cooking. You could say I was practically born in the kitchen." She giggled nervously and stopped when she saw I wasn't laughing. "I'll make a great server because I know how to do the job so well. Besides, I excel in customer service." She flashed a charming smile and flipped her long brown hair to one shoulder.

I raised an eyebrow at her creativity and played her little game. "Really? Your experience in the food business sounds promising. I suppose you could be the right fit for the position. I'll ask only one more question and then your interview will be finished. What's the name of the restaurant you worked for?"

The confidence in her face faded. She fidgeted with the salt shaker in her hands and dropped it. "Its name? Uh . . . The Sand Dollar. Yeah, it was called The Sand Dollar."

"The Sand Dollar? Hmm, I've never heard of that restaurant before. Is it in GlenPoint?"

"No. I mean—yes! It was open a few years ago, but then it went out of business. My father passed away, and our family couldn't run it anymore. We were unable to pay the rent and had to close its doors."

"Oh, how tragic. I'm sorry for your loss." I let out my breath in disgust and slowly shook my head. To embellish one's qualifications for employment was one thing, but to lie about a father's death was simply repulsive. A beautiful woman who lacked discretion was like a ring of gold in a swine's snout.

"Yes, it was a difficult time for us all. It still is, actually. That's why I really need this job. I can help support my mother and pay our rent. She's been out of work for a while now, and—"

I looked down at my watch and quickly stood to my feet. The reservoir of falsehoods was entertaining, but there was only so much I could bear. I handed her back her application and smiled. "I wish you and your family the best, Sandra. I'm sorry, but I don't think you're right for the position. Thank you for applying at La Mer."

A puzzled look crossed her face, and she slowly raised from her chair. She looked at the paper in her hand as if she didn't know how it got there. "That's it? You've just decided it? Are you the manager here? Or is there someone else who does the hiring? I just want to make sure that I'm talking to the right person." She looked around the club to find someone of authority.

"You're talking to the right person."

"How do I know that? Who's the owner? I think they need a chance to take a look at my application." She waved her paper madly in my face.

"I'm the owner."

She dropped her hand to her side. The furrows in her forehead deepened as she scanned my face for deception. The lies she told were a habit, and she automatically assumed everyone she interacted with was dishonest like herself. After seeing that I wasn't wavering from my decision, she slung her purse over her shoulder and tucked her application inside. "I don't know why I didn't get the position. I think I'm very qualified for the job. Are you sure there isn't anything I can do to change your mind? You know, answer more questions or something?" She popped her shoulder in just the right way to allow for her pink oversized sweater to fall to one side. Her creamy white skin glowed under a beam of recess lightening. She puckered her painted lips and smiled at the change in my expression.

I knew what she was implying, and I didn't bother to hide my approval. It didn't take much for the gears to change in our conversation. Her advances to placate my rejection were disgusting, and if it had been at an earlier time in my life, I would've declined without hesitation. But the morality of my soul was decaying as the appetite of my flesh was growing stronger.

She gave me one last smile and turned on her heel for the exit. I pulled at the collar of my shirt and followed her like a lamb to the slaughter.

Chapter Seven

I dove into a large approaching wave and pulled the leash of my surfboard with me. The long pink oval danced across the surface of the water like a kite being pulled on a string. I powered through the foamy waves that rolled through the surf zone and stopped when the ocean became placid. Settling with an awkward flop, I draped my torso over the top of the board and turned toward the shore. My heart thundered painfully in my chest as I scanned the stretch of sand for the visitors. A total of six young males were suited to surf. One of them walked to the water.

I checked my waist to make sure my scales weren't visible and pulled at the hem of my top. My skin felt sweaty under the rubbery material that seemed to be a magnet to the sun's hot rays. And it didn't help that my hands couldn't stop shaking. I feared the idea of interacting with a human—especially one

I was planning to kill. I stretched my neckline to get a bit of airflow and took in a raspy breath.

"Don't forget to breathe," Sabrina whispered from behind me.

I flinched at the sound of her voice and slid into the water. The board's long shadow cast above my head as I took in as much air as I could. After taking a few deep breaths, I broke through the sparkling surface and scowled at the mermaid at my side. "Don't scare me like that. I already have enough anxiety as it is. Besides, I thought you were upset with me . . . calling me a bloody fool and all." My wetsuit squeaked as I slid across the board.

"I was mad. You took too long to follow me to the shore. But I'm not anymore. I wanted to wish you luck in trapping a human. The gods must be happy because we haven't had surfers come here in a long time." She frowned and traced her finger along the black and white flower pattern that decorated the board's edges. "You're bound to snare a man. Just keep telling yourself you're perfect. Otherwise, he will detect your insecurity and take a position of control."

I thanked Sabrina for her advice and tried my best to appear calm. Five out of the six swimmers had already begun to surf. We floated from a distance and watched as they waded through the breaking water and rode the curl of waves back to the shore. The last one suited up and ran to join the others.

"What if I'm too far back? I mean, they're over there, and I'm floating back here. What if they don't notice me?"

"They'll notice you. You don't want to swim any closer or you're likely to get pounded by the waves. At that point, you would have to actually use your surfboard. Unless that's what you're going for—a mermaid who knows how to surf."

I shook my head at the thought and chuckled. "No thanks. I think I'll stick to being seen as a human. If I'm seen, that is." I considered my future encounter and began the primping routine I did every time I went out on a date. I smoothed back my hair to look pretty around my face and picked off the algae from my top. After adjusting my position to get a better grip on my board, I pulled back my shoulders to accentuate my curves and faced my potential suitors. It was hard getting ready without the use of a mirror, but it was the best I could do.

"You don't have to do that, Gwendolyn. You're perfect. From the crown of your head to the tip of your tail, you're flawlessly designed. It doesn't matter how hard the wind blows because your hair will never be out of place. You'll never have dry lips or blemishes on your skin. You'll always look better than everyone else. You just have to know it in your heart. Empty the negativity that has obscured your perception and fill yourself with pride."

A male suddenly broke from the group and swam toward our location. His red surfboard vanished beneath a large, foamy wave and reappeared a bit closer.

Sabrina shook my arm with a squeal. "It worked! It worked! My plan to use a surfboard worked. If only I decided to try it out first."

I waited for him to turn around and ride a wave back to shore, but he continued to head in our direction. He said something to someone nearby and pointed to where we floated. I nearly ducked in response.

"This is it," Sabrina whispered. "Make every moment count. Just remember what I told you. Be prideful. Don't let him take control of the situation." She gave my arm a parting squeeze and disappeared beneath the surface.

A gentle breeze blew across the waves, and my board dipped and swayed. I clutched the bobbing device so hard my knuckles showed bone. The tremble that plagued my hands returned, and the pulse in my ears roared. It was absurd to think I was so scared to talk to a human. One would think I was the victim and he was the monster.

The male began to pick up speed.

My skin broke out in a cold sweat. I closed my eyes and tried to calm my heart. The words of Sabrina repeated themselves over and over in my head.

"Fill yourself with pride. Fill yourself with pride. Fill yourself with pride. You're perfect. You're perfect. You're perfect."

"Hey! Are you okay over there?!" A male's voice rang out in the distance.

"You're perfect. You're perfect. You're perfect."

"Hello! I said, are you okay?! Do you need help?!"

"You're perfect. You're perfect. You're perfect."

"Do you need help getting back to shore? Miss? Are you okay?"

"You're perfect."

The coward, Gwendolyn, who trembled with insecurity and fear fled at that moment and pride himself entered my being. He was too powerful for me to resist. He was an unforeseen force, a life-changing authority, proposing to rewrite the very code of what made me, me. He knocked on the door of my heart. He spoke great swelling words of flattery. I harkened and opened my door. His company was welcomed. His presence was alluring and sensual. He took me by the hand and lifted me up. He set my eyes on pleasurable things. He set my eyes on myself. I gave him my will, and we became one. He burned deep within me.

I'm perfect.

I opened my eyes completely calm and confident. A breathless individual treaded water several feet from my location. He was an attractive male, no older than twenty. His tan, muscular body clung to a surfboard that read LIFEGUARD across the top. He slicked back his blonde hair that fell to his chin and blinked his blue eyes in concern. A look of wonder quickly spread across his face as he took in the goddess who floated before him.

"Are you okay, miss?"

"I'm perfect," I breathed. I met his trailing eyes and enjoyed his obvious carnality. A wash of red came over his face. I smiled and purred, "Why? Did I do something wrong?"

He continued to stare at my lips even though they had stopped moving. He swallowed and shook his head. "No. But you've been floating beyond the surf zone for quite some time now. I didn't know if you needed help getting back to shore." He pulled his eyes from my face and glanced over my shoulder. "Are you here alone? I could've sworn I saw someone with you."

"I'm alone."

"Hmm, that's funny. I thought I saw someone floating next to you." He scanned the horizon and shrugged his shoulders. "But I guess that would be impossible since I didn't see them with a surfboard. The swim back to shore would be pretty difficult. Say, why are you surfing out this far?"

My eyes burrowed deep into his. He became uncomfortable and looked away. I pushed at the water with both hands, and my board drifted closer. I grinned, conscious of my full lips. "I like to swim past the surf zone and float where the water is calm. The movement of the waves is relaxing. It seems to get my mind off of things." I gave my tail a hard flap and erected high enough for him to see my flawless torso.

His eyes nearly fell out of their sockets. He closed his mouth and cleared his throat. "Yes. I know exactly what you're talking about. I love laying out on my board, too. I can't tell you how many times I come here and do just that." He grunted and lifted himself to a sitting position. His muscular abdomen flexed as his legs straddled his board for stability. "I'm Brandon, by the way. Or Bran for short. Or B. man if you're really close."

"My name's Gwendolyn."

"Gwendolyn . . ." he repeated slowly. "Wow. Okay, cool. Nice to meet you, Gwen. Can I call you that?"

I nodded my head.

"Cool. I've met a lot of people at my post, but I haven't seen you before." He paused for a moment and pretended to monitor the swimming group of individuals he shamelessly neglected. He turned back to me and beamed. "Do you come here often?"

I found an indistinct area in the distance and pointed to it. "I usually go further down the shore if I want to surf. It seems to be less crowded over there."

He looked in my pointed finger's direction and laughed. "Less crowded? By the pier? You've got to be kidding me. You'd be lucky to catch a wave that doesn't crash into some five-year-old learning how to swim. Everyone and their mother goes there." He hooked his hands behind his head and purposely flexed his arms. I raised an eyebrow to fake interest. "My lifeguard station has been pretty dead lately. And when I say dead, I mean dead. No one comes here anymore. In fact, my friends surfing today have been the first group to visit in months. So, if you want to find a new spot to surf, or float as you call it, this might be the place for you. If I'm at my post, I'll guarantee to keep you safe." He flung a piece of seaweed off his board and flexed his arms again.

I looked past his showy brawn and focused on the throbbing pulse that bulged in his neck. He was nervous. That much was obvious. It was proof I had complete control over our encounter. The pride that burned deep within my heart exploded into flames.

I paddled in the water until my board was side to side with his. He saw me up close and almost toppled over.

"I'd love to surf at your post," I cooed. "If it isn't as crowded as you say. These guys surfing now, are they your friends?" I looked at the busy shore and coughed discreetly in my hand. The simple exercise of idle chit-chat was depleting my reservoirs of air.

"Oh, yeah. They're real good buddies of mine. There's Juan, over there drying off. Chase is the guy who just rode that wave back to shore. Andrew's head is floating right over . . . there. Tray—wow! Tray just ate it! Poor guy. Alexander . . . hmm . . . is probably taking a leak or something because I can't see him. And Joey, okay, he should be easy to spot since he has hot pink hair. He's swimming right over there." He pointed to a male floating near our location and remarked about his hopeless addiction for tattoos. The individual turned in our direction as if he knew we were talking about him.

My blood grew cold in my veins, and I looked the other way. It was Ryan's best friend, Joey. The memories I made within his company had all at once hit me square between the eyes. The taco runs. The movie nights. The bonfire parties at the beach. The recollections that took nearly six months to suppress all came flooding back in less than a second.

"Are you okay? You look like you just saw a ghost."

I opened my mouth to speak, but exploded in a torrent of coughs. Brandon reached for my board to steady it.

"Whoa, are you feeling okay? Take a deep breath. Take a deep breath."

"I'm okay," I sputtered, coughing again. "I must've swallowed a bug or something. I'll be fine."

"Are you sure? You look pale, and your breath sounds a little raspy. Maybe you should follow me back to the shore. I can introduce you to my friends and—"

"No." I shook my head and promptly declined. The safety of my existence would be threatened if Joey recognized who I was. I couldn't even swim in his vicinity. I suddenly wished I gave Brandon a fake name. "No, I'm fine. Really. It's just an itchy throat. That's all. Honest."

"Are you sure?"

"Yes."

"Hmm . . . well, okay. If you're sure you're alright. I hate to leave so soon, but I better get back to my post. What good is a lifeguard who's floating in the water?" He chuckled anxiously and scratched the back of his neck. His voice cracked, and he cleared his throat. "But, hey. Uh, I was thinking. If you're not too busy . . . uh . . . would you like to hang out after my shift? I'll be off in about an hour or so. There's a party that we're headed to out in GlenPoint Ridge. Juan got accepted into GPU, and his parents are gone for the weekend. It's your typical thrasher. You know—big house, loud music. But I'm sure we can find a quiet place to get to know one another."

I bit the inside of my cheek to keep from coughing. My lungs ached within my chest, and my throat closed tight. I didn't care about taking his soul anymore. I just wanted to breathe. I mustered up as much air as I could and nodded. "That sounds like a lot of fun, but I'm afraid I can't make it." I sputtered and bit down on my cheek harder. "I would love to see you again. Maybe we can meet here?"

My voiced interest was the perfect distraction from my silent suffocation. His face beamed with joy. "Really? That would be awesome! I'll be out of town for the rest of this month, but I'll be back on the first. Will that work?"

I nodded and gasped.

"Do you want to meet at my post? Lifeguard station twelve? It's an easy place to find and—"

"No. Let's meet here in the water."

"Really? Okay, cool. Same time?"

I nodded and coughed again. I needed to breathe so bad I wanted to drop in the water and forgo all formalities of parting. But there was one thing I needed to ask that required my last remaining strength. I could barely whisper. "What is the date today?"

"What's the date? It's August the thirteenth."

"See you on the first of September. Goodbye, Brandon." I took in a chesty breath and forced myself to smile. I was hoping my prompt dismissal would encourage him to leave.

He reluctantly took my cue and positioned himself across his board. A look of total adoration crossed his face as he gave me one last glance. "I don't think it was by chance that we met today," he stammered. "I can't wait to get to know you better. I hope you have a nice day floating." He gave me a sheepish grin and sped off toward the shore.

When I was certain he was gone, I promptly released my surfboard and sank beneath the surface. My heart filled with elation while my lungs filled with water. The freedom that seemed impossible to obtain was dangling in my face. The whole time I interacted with my victim, I could detect the distinct taste Sabrina told me to look for. She said love tasted like salt. Who would've guessed it was so easy to obtain? I grinned with utter triumph and surfaced for my board. I couldn't wait for September first to come. Brandon's soul was ready for the taking.

Chapter Eight

I took a deep breath from my cigarette and winced from the burn in my lungs. A thin wisp of smoke floated from my mouth and dissipated in the moonlit air. If one was to become relaxed from the act of smoking, I certainly wasn't doing something right. If anything, it was making me feel jittery. I put the smoldering object between my lips and took another uncomfortable drag. A gust of wind blew across the shore, and the ash that dangled from my cigarette flew to my shirt. I wiped away the crumbly mess and extinguished its burning tip in the sand. At least it was one less vice that held me captive. Heaven only knew I had too many. A foamy wave spilled across my path, drenching my leather shoes and taking my failed stump of tobacco with it.

My chest filled deep with a heavy sigh as I watched the surf rise and fall in the darkness. If only a wave could carry away my troubles. Here I stood, one of the most successful men in all of GlenPoint, yet I was miserable at best. I had everything a human could ever want. My club made more revenue than all the other businesses in town. My garage housed two luxury sports cars. My closet overflowed with expensive clothing. My apartment was arrayed with the finest furniture. Whatever my eyes desired, I did not keep from them. Only, my eyes were never satisfied. My soul was not content with what this world had to offer. I acquired a great amount, but I was in need of more. The void could never be filled. I grasped and grasped and grasped, and all was vanity and grasping for the wind.

I looked for the smoothest rock in the horseshoe formation and slowly took a seat. It was odd that I gravitated to the one place that caused so much pain. A long night of self-reflection, and I wind up at the beach. Perhaps it was within my nature to return to the place where it started. The ocean was all I ever knew. I remembered so many countless nights looking at the world from the opposite end of the shore. I wanted nothing more than to become a human. I imagined a life filled with companionship, joy, and hearty laughter—not the meaningless caresses of infatuated women.

A large wave crashed against the rocks, and a torrent of water flowed into the basin around me. I reached into the frothy pool and grasped a pink scalloped shell that floated on the surface. My hand closed around the sharp object until it cut my skin and broke. There was one victory I could claim in my pursuit of spiritual deterioration—I never allowed a relationship with Avangeline. Try as she might, and she tried often, I could not become intimate with her again. Maybe it was her debased mind that turned my stomach sour, or perhaps it was the horrible kiss we shared the first night I got drunk. Whatever it was, no matter how intoxicated I became, she would never be allowed to touch my mouth again.

Shadows played with moonlight on the water. A seal's head appeared above a white-crested wave and bobbed with the change of current. I unraveled the tie that squeezed around my neck and stuffed it in the back pocket of my slacks. I needed a fresh start. I needed to move from GlenPoint and begin a life somewhere completely different. If only I could erase the memories in my mind. I could pack my belongings and flee to a different city, but how would I ignore the tragedy in my wake? How do I forget the poor decisions that appeared in my reflection? If only there was an answer.

The animal that lingered from a distance had drawn unusually close. It wove its way through the choppy surf zone and stopped where the water met the shore. I lifted my head from my hands and squinted to get a better view of its form. Its silhouette didn't look like a seal's. It had a small head atop a narrow neck and a cape-like shadow that could possibly be hair. Its quick movements and long strides didn't look like the swimming pattern of a seal either. A powerful wave struck the area where it floated. It disappeared beneath the water and pushed through the swell to resurface.

I chuckled at the obvious call of duty and quickly unbuttoned the cuffs of my shirt. If the creature was a human, they certainly had a death wish. Only a fool would overlook the dangers of a changing tide. It looked like a late night rescue may be in order.

They suddenly rose high out of the water and two pale arms emerged in the darkness. I jumped to my feet and gawked in utter astonishment. It was a human! There was no doubt about it. Their perfected breaststroke appeared to be more leisure than peril. But why would someone swim so late in the night? It was at least one or two in the morning. And the water was too cold to enjoy without a wetsuit, which clearly they weren't wearing. Unless it was a mermaid taking a midnight swim under the stars. In that case, the whole scenario made perfect sense. The longer I stood and watched them maneuver the wiles of the ocean, the more I knew exactly what they were. A human could never withstand such turbulent tides.

They sank beneath the surface and reappeared closer.

I dropped to one knee and tried my best to blend in with the rocks. At that moment, I was grateful I wore all black. The shore had a bit of a haze, so I was sure they didn't see me. I slid to the sand and crouched between two rocks to be sure. A narrow crevasse provided the perfect view of the breaking water. I pressed my face against the cold, wet surface and waited for the aquatic guest to appear.

The water collected and spilled its contents. The waves spread across the sand and returned to where they came. I checked the time on my watch and yawned with a tired stretch. If it was a romantic rendezvous I stumbled upon, the couple planned their passion a little late. An hour chosen to hide the mermaid's form and pending murder, no doubt. I looked around the shore to find the unlucky human in question. No one was to be found.

I drummed my fingers against the rock and cracked the back of my neck. Another wave came in and poured over my shoes. I hissed with growing frustration and bent at my waist to untie them. They were officially ruined. My socks were drenched. My feet were cold and numb. I was a total idiot for wasting my time at the beach. Here I hid, hoping to catch a glimpse of some insignificant individual, when I could be fast asleep in bed. And for what? Why would I want to meddle in someone's ill-fated affair? I didn't need the uncomfortable obligation to help a fellow human in need. Not to mention the haunting visual that would conjure my own checkered past. Such calamity was none of my business. It was best if I suppressed my curiosity and made my way back home.

I wrung the water out from my socks and slung my shoes over my shoulder. I turned from my departure and took one last look to the shore.

Gwendolyn surfaced.

I felt my face drain of color. I pressed hard against the rock and took an uncomfortable, dry swallow.

It was her!

She was alive. I could not believe my eyes. She never suffocated the night she transformed. I assumed for so long that she never survived in her new environment. To see her slithering up the sand was an image I couldn't comprehend. It was as if I watched an illusion. I cleared away the seaweed that blocked my vision and stuck my face deep into the crevasse. It took every ounce of self-control not to jump over my barricade and make my presence known.

A large wave crashed against the shore, and a blanket of foam spread across her pathway. Her greenish-gray tail glittered with water as it pushed and slithered behind her erected torso. Large pieces of driftwood littered the area where she traveled, posing an annoying predicament for an appendage that couldn't climb. The obstacle didn't seem to faze her. She mechanically cleared away the debris as if she had done it so many times before. The steady bending and throwing transitioned from methodical to almost frantic until she reached a small cave-like opening in the rocks. I wedged myself within the cleft to get a better view of her location.

Her body suddenly became stiff, and she dropped the wood she was holding. She nervously looked over her shoulder and scanned the dark shore. Her large eyes darted from the lifeguard station, to the pier, and then settled on where I hid. Her stare locked with mine, and I nearly choked on my tongue. I forgot how beautiful she was. Her long blonde hair was swept to one side, revealing a flawless female torso that glowed in the moonlight. Every feature of her angelic face was perfect—from the round of her cheeks, to the curve of her nose, to the scarlet of her lips. Her forehead knotted in a furrow, and a look of concern swept over her expression. A car's horn sounded from the highway, and she craned her neck to survey the parking lot. After a tense minute of gauging the area and seeing no one threatened her privacy, she removed the last remaining driftwood that blocked the cave's entrance and quickly disappeared inside.

I couldn't stand it any longer. I pulled out from my concealment in the crevice and climbed over the barricade of rocks. It was a miracle I stumbled upon her presence. The chances of seeing her again were next to none. I couldn't let her leave.

I sprinted across the sand with legs that felt like lead. My foot caught on a piece of wood, and I stumbled to keep from falling. She exited the cave with her back turned toward me.

I approached her location as she dragged an object from the rocks. She spun in my direction and stifled a scream.

"Gwendolyn, hi!" My voice cracked with excitement, and I coughed to conceal it. I struggled to catch my breath. "How are you? What a surprise running into you tonight."

Her face instantly paled in what appeared to be a mixture of bafflement and horror. She slithered back a few paces and looked over her shoulder.

I spread my hands in her direction to show her I meant no harm. "I'm not going to hurt you. It's me, Marcus. Don't you remember who I am?" I reached to hold her hand, but she recoiled at the gesture. A gust of wind blew across her hair, and the icy blonde tendrils that fell to her waist swept behind her shoulders. She made no effort to cover her exposed breasts. I struggled not to stare. "We met on this shore. I saved you from drowning on those rocks over there. Don't you remember our disastrous first date? It ended with a slap." I peered behind her rigid body and saw a surfboard and wetsuit laying in the sand. Her late night belongings didn't make any sense. And her bizarre amnesia to my presence was becoming painfully awkward. I let out an irritated sigh and crossed my arms across my chest. I didn't understand. "Don't you remember me?"

Her eyes scanned my face with persistent confusion. I thrust my hands in my pockets and looked the other way. I wasn't going to be made to look like a fool. If her oxygen-deprived brain lost all memory of our relationship, my continual demand for its recognition wasn't going to bring it back. Only a desperate individual would probe any further. I was excited at the thought of revisiting our relationship, but not at the cost of my self-respect.

I groaned in irritation. "I'm sorry if my presence makes you so uncomfortable. I'm glad to see you're still alive. Well, it's getting pretty late. I better go . . ."

"No, wait!" she blurted out, catching me by the hand. The touch of her velvet skin sent shivers up my arms. "Of course, I remember you. How could I forget? I'm sorry I didn't answer right away, but you caught me by surprise. It's just been so long and . . ." She pulled me to herself and offered an apologetic smile. "How've you been? Do you still own La Mer? How's Avangeline been managing? As a human, of course."

My eyebrow arched, and I gave a halfhearted chuckle. Impossible! The loss of her memory had returned to the detail. "I should be the one asking you how you're doing. Thanks for the concern, though. I still own La Mer, and Avangeline is getting along okay. She's obnoxious to have around, but that should change soon." I bristled at the thought of her sleeping on my couch and scrambled to change the subject. I didn't want anything to spoil our conversation. I quickly shifted gears. "How've you been? I'm so relieved to see you're still alive. There hasn't been a day that's gone by that I haven't thought about your safety." My smile slowly faded as I considered her hostile environment.

She bit her lower lip and unflinchingly held my stare. Her gunmetal eyes, still crescent from smiling, slowly filled with tears. A haunting look of despair pulled at her countenance, and her gaze drifted to the ground. It was within that quiet moment that I felt a total gut-wrenching empathy for her loss. She was staring at my feet.

"I'm not doing very well," she whispered, barely audible above the waves. "I haven't been able to accept the fact that I'm a mermaid. I think that's the hardest part, you know? Coming to grips with what I've become. I've lost everything. My family. My friends. Even the simple things in life, like talking, are gone." Her hand released mine as her eyes remained fixed on the ground. I dug my toes deep in the sand and suddenly wished I put back on my shoes.

Her tiny voice cut through the silence. "I'm not used to living alone. The solitude is unbearable. Every day I wake up in a cold, watery hell and no one knows where I am. I might as well be dead. I'm sure that's what my family thinks. That's what you thought, right?" She wiped her face with the back of her hand and looked for my response.

I sighed in growing discomfort and tried to avoid her stare. The pain of her absence was still too fresh. "Yes, I thought you died. I didn't think you could learn how to breathe. I wish I would've explained how your new lungs worked, but your transformation happened so fast. I was overcome with shock. By the time I realized you could be suffocating, I was driving up the street. It was too late for me to help." I met her glistening eyes and looked the other way. My absence in her transformation was a regret I could never shake.

"Well, I made it. I learned to breathe, thankfully. But it wasn't easy. There was a moment where I was certain I would die. I remember my lungs squeezed so tight I could taste blood." She turned her face and winced at the memory. "I took a long look at the water and saw that my oxygen wasn't coming from the right place. I knew I had to do something that went against my instincts."

"And I'm so glad you did! You were given the anatomy of a fish, and you figured it out. Your first breath underwater was probably frightening. That says a lot about who you are and the hope you should have for your future. Managing to stay alive is half the battle." My eyes ran across the pink surfboard that hid behind her. "That surfboard and wetsuit over there—did you meet someone?"

She barely gave them a glance and shrugged her shoulders. "These? No. They weren't given to me. I found them on the shore. I wear the wetsuit and float across the board in hopes to see someone I know."

"You mean . . ." I swallowed dryly. "You mean you haven't met anyone? You haven't met a man yet?" My eyes wandered back to the board and stopped. I didn't want to know. I couldn't imagine her in the arms of someone else.

She muttered something about her future and shook her head. "Are you talking about entrapping a human? How could I? I can't bring myself to murder. I want my old life again, but not at the expense of taking someone else's. I just can't do that."

The muscles in my stomach unclenched as an invisible weight was lifted. Despite the perverse world that she was thrust into, her morality remained miraculously unspoiled.

Her breath became raspy, and she coughed. "I just want my situation to change. Day after day, I pray to see my friends and family. But no one ever comes. It's like I'm living in a nightmare. I want to wake up and eat a pancake breakfast with my parents. I want to watch cable and call my friends to hang out. I want to walk through my backyard and feel the grass beneath my feet. I can't tell you how many times I've dreamt about my life on land. But it's only a memory. My nineteen years of life have been reduced to a handful of memories, and it feels like they're fading. It's getting harder and harder for me to remember what I had." Her face reddened, and she turned away. It took a torturous minute for her to continue. "I'm lonely," she mouthed. "I need someone to talk to. I think I could get through my days if I knew someone was there."

I reached for her chin and tenderly tilted her face toward mine. A tear streamed down her cheek, and I wiped it away. I wanted to hold her. I wanted to smooth back her hair and tell her all that was in my heart. But time was running out. Her hand made a cup over her mouth, and she gave a throaty cough. She would need to return to the ocean to breathe.

"You can talk to me," I whispered, tucking a strand of hair behind her ear. "I will always be here for you. We'll figure this thing out. If there's another way to transform you into a human, I promise I'll find out what it is. Just don't give up. Don't give up hope. That's what makes you so beautiful, Gwendolyn. It's your heart. It's the integrity you possess that's absent in so many people. Don't do something you know you shouldn't do. Remain strong in what you believe is right."

She reached for my hands and pulled me to herself. Her body brushed against mine, and my heart instantly picked up speed. "Thank you," she said, blinking away another tear. "I'll take your advice. There are times when I think about entrapping, but I know it's a bad thought. I can't kill a man. I just get desperate sometimes." She let out a wheezy breath and forced a smile. The pupils in her eyes opened to complete black. "Thank you for listening to my troubles. It feels so good to have you in my life."

"It's my pleasure," I breathed, reaching for the back of her head. I wove my fingers through her hair and held a fistful of her tendrils. The delicate smell of beach rose, vanilla, and musk made my mouth water. "I will never leave your side."

Her arms circled around my back as her face slowly approached mine. The warmth of her body could be felt through my shirt. My heart hammered in my chest.

"Are you nervous?" she questioned, giving me a small smile. Her full lips brushed softly against mine. "You're trembling a little."

"Yes, I am. I could never imagine this moment would happen. I don't want it to end."

"Who says it has to end?"

Our lips slowly brushed again.

She pressed her mouth hard against mine in a kiss. My body broke out in gooseflesh as my lips covered hers. Her mouth was sweet and delicate. Her eyelashes fluttered softly as I reached to hold her face. Her hands smoothed the length of my back and pressed my body against hers. My muscles became weak, and my legs bent at the knees. She uttered a soft moan and pressed her lips harder. She grasped my upper arms and pulled me to herself. She held me so hard she dug her nails into my shirt. The pain from her fingers was scarcely noticed through my blinding haze of ecstasy.

All at once, her body became stiff, and she pulled away from my face. She looked to her surfboard and recoiled.

"What's wrong?" I asked, stunned from our abrupt stop. "Why are you looking at me like that?"

Her eyes raked my face in seeming abhorrence. They narrowed to thin slits. "You didn't do anything wrong."

"Yeah? Then why do you look so upset? "

"I'm not," she sputtered, breaking into a cough. She bent to the sand and grasped the surfboard's leash and wetsuit. "I need to go. I'm running out of air."

"Okay, I get that. But why did you end our kiss so fast? Why do you look angry and confused? Something made you upset." I reached for my forearm and gave it a dull rub. The wound she left was suddenly beginning to hurt.

"It's getting late, and I need to go. It was nice seeing you, Marcus. I hope you have a good night."

I continued to hold my injury as I studied her myriad of expressions. She was angry and confused, but most disturbingly, she was disappointed. The realization of her corruption punched me right in the face. I rubbed the side of my arm and winced. "You were trying to kill me."

Her head snapped in my direction. "What?"

"You were trying to kill me."

"What do you mean? I wasn't trying to kill you."

"You were pressing your face against mine because you were expecting for me to release my soul. That's why you look so disappointed. It's because you didn't transform."

She gasped for a breath and dropped her surfboard's leash and wetsuit. A vein bulged in her neck that was visible from where I stood. "I told you, I'm running out of air. I need to go, or I will suffocate."

"You can't lie. I can see right through you."

Her eyes darted from my face to the ocean. I almost expected for her to push past me and make an exit for the shore. But she didn't. She just stood there in confusion, not knowing whether to stay or go.

"What's the point of your facade? You were expecting to transform, right? You were thinking I was going to crumble into ash and wash away with the first wave. I know what you're trying to do. Stop pretending."

"You tasted like salt," she said bluntly.

"And?"

"True love tastes like salt. I thought you were ready to give up your soul."

"True love doesn't taste like salt. Who told you that?"

"Yes, it does," she insisted, ignoring my question. "I just don't understand why I didn't change. Everything appeared to be right."

"Did you think I could give you something I took for myself? You will have to find a soul in a human. As for true love, you don't need it to acquire a soul. Lust and love are used interchangeably. The googly-eyed idiot that drools over your figure will do just fine." I paused to look at the water. The exposure of my vulnerability struck an unforeseen chord. I took a deep breath and let it out slowly. "True love is something difficult to find. Dare I say, impossible. It's something I've never obtained. I've heard it's wonderful. Something possibly too wonderful for a wretch like me to experience."

"Don't talk to me about true love," she snapped. "I know what it is."

"Do you? Well, I don't. I've heard it's patient. I've heard it's kind and selfless. It isn't easily angered or rude. It's something that will compel someone to lay down their life to save the life of another. Do you know what that is?" I tore my eyes from the ocean to get a good look at her face. Her expression was twisted in unsuppressed rage. "I don't truly love you, Gwendolyn. What you taste from me is lust."

"Lust?" She bit her lower lip and frowned. "But I thought. . ." She started to argue her point, but decided against it. She coughed and shook her head in visible defeat. "Well, that explains why I didn't transform. Thank you for clarifying things. This mermaid life is really difficult to understand."

She bent to the sand and grabbed her leash and wetsuit. She swept back her hair and smirked. "Well, I better go before I run out of air. It was nice seeing—"

I lifted my hand to stop her. "Save your pleasantries for your victim. I don't want to hear any more of your garbage. Heaven help you, Gwendolyn."

She nodded without saying another word and quickly slithered to the shore.

Chapter Nine

Days passed like months. Every morning when I surfaced, I hoped my victim would return. Lifeguard station twelve flourished with visitors, but Brandon was nowhere to be seen. His absence for the month appeared to be true. Still, Sabrina and I shared the wetsuit and surfboard in hopes to trap a passerby. I had a few close encounters that lifted my spirits briefly. An old man boating with his dog almost approached my location. A male surfing with his girlfriend watched me from afar. A pair of young men swam close as they taught their friend to windsurf. Every day brought the potential of another entrapment, but nothing ever succeeded. My hope remained in the promise of my victim's return. I counted the days of his reappearance with a pile of calendar stones. I dropped the seventh to the mound, making the date August twentieth. I had eleven days left to wait. Eleven days until our anticipated date. My heart leapt with elation while I rearranged the pile. I could almost taste the salt of his adoration as I imagined his lips touching mine. I stuffed a piece of kelp in my mouth and recited a little prayer.

"Morning star,
Beauty divine,
Grant me your favor,
To take what is mine.

Infinite power,
Possessor of keys,
Shine from the heavens,
And I will be set free."

A current of water swept through my pile of rocks, and one rolled away. I frowned at its annoying departure and found a larger replacement. The smooth stone moved with little effort as I pushed it to the others. I assessed the mound that erected from the sand and slowly nodded. Yes, my pile was growing by the day. I would soon walk from this cursed shore and live my life as it once was. My time would finally come.

I lifted my eyes with great pride and repeated my little prayer. The words seemed to bounce off the surface of the water and fall to the ocean's floor. I shook my head with growing discouragement and plucked another piece of kelp. I knew better than to ask a silly star for help. Here I was, calling upon the gods of the earth when I was a god myself! It didn't make any sense. I had the power to ensnare anyone I wanted. To ask an entity for assistance was as good as admitting defeat. I recanted my foolish supplication and revised a better rhyme.

"Morning star,
Ruler of sky,
Why has your light grown dim?
You hide your face with jealous eyes,
For my beauty will always win."

A high-pitched squeal sounded throughout the water. I turned my head in the direction of the surface just as the shadow of a panicked baby whale passed. The long silhouette of an adult bull shark followed close behind him. I looked around for any sign of the whale's pod and saw none. The infant was most likely separated from his mother to be eaten. If she was dead, the creature would be rendered defenseless.

The hungry shark that lingered in the recesses began to pick up speed. He turned in a large semi-circle and closed the gap to his prey. The helpless whale screamed in terror and turned in my direction.

I smiled at the silent challenge and cracked the back of my neck. Sharks were respected amongst merfolk as a savage entity to be left alone. To instigate violence against such an animal would require skill. If anything, it was a quarrel Sabrina never took on. She didn't have the nerve. She repeated countless stories of mermaids who fought to preserve their territory only to be ripped to shreds in a few seconds. It was an altercation that opposed my good judgement. But as badly as I wanted to swim away and let nature be nature, I was infuriated with the unfair match.

It seemed unjust to pit an infant against a monster. And more importantly, I was hungry—so hungry in fact that rubbery vegetation or the thin meat of crab wasn't going to suffice. I thirsted for the blood of a much larger prey. And this was my moment! The whale screamed again, and I gave my tail a hard flap.

The shark hardly noticed as I approached him from behind. His smooth, muscular body flexed, and he lunged forward. He grasped his prey by the edge of his fin and thrashed violently for the kill. A shrill cry filled my ears. I pushed through the cloud of coppery red and located the two rows of gills that were found behind the shark's eyes. My fingers reached deep into the pillowy crevasses, and I pulled as hard as I could. The tearing of flesh released a haze of bright red. The confused predator spun around to find his opponent. In the corner of my eye, I saw the baby escape into a forest of kelp. I smiled and grasped the thrashing shark's head with both hands. Using my thumbs, I covered his large black eyes and pushed in hard. Warm jelly oozed out of his sockets and covered my hands. The blind enemy spun around in circles, signaling his defeat.

"Hey! What's going on here?" Sabrina appeared from the kelp and smirked at the glorious catch. *"Impressive! Did you kill him, or was he already dying?"*

I snatched the shark's whipping tail and pulled it to my mouth. His skin felt sandpapery and thick. I dragged my lips to a soft divot near his rear dorsal fin and sank my teeth in. The metallic taste of warm blood sent shivers down my spine.

"I killed him," I boasted, tearing another mouthful. I swallowed the chewy morsel and turned so I could get a

good look at Sabrina's expression. She was shocked. *"I killed him, and I hardly lifted a finger. It's quite simple, actually. I heard once that if you get attacked by a shark to grab them by their gills or their eyes. I happened to do both. He didn't stand a chance. Better said, he was toast."*

"Toast? What's toast?"

I laughed and took another bite of the beast. Toast? I hardly remembered the stuff.

***

Avangeline's heeled boot stepped over my face as she crossed into the dark kitchen of my apartment. She threw her purse on the counter with a heavy sigh and tied back the mass of auburn curls that fell to the middle of her back. Her cell phone beeped quietly and she opened it, revealing a grin of triumph by the light of the display screen. After typing out a quick response to the caller's message, she stuffed the cell phone into the front pocket of her slacks and opened the door of the refrigerator. She pushed around the excess of take-out boxes and partially used condiment bottles before reluctantly settling on a half-eaten carton of tuna sashimi. Satisfied with her selection, she walked back to my motionless body and stepped over it, entering the moonlit living room. She took her seat by the window and slowly opened her prize.

"Were you going to eat any of this?" she asked, taking in a deep whiff. She carefully inspected a small piece of fish before popping it in her mouth.

"No," I uttered, attempting to prop up on both elbows. The forced range of motion sent a pain down my neck, landing me back to the ground in defeat. Her ravenous slurping echoed loudly across the room.

"So, who's the master tonight, Marcus? Scotch? Whiskey? That half-drunk bottle of wine I brought home from work?" Her eyes wandered to the empty bottle lying at my side and narrowed. "I was going to use that for my date with Lance. I guess I'll have to swipe another after my shift." She swallowed the morsel she chewed and gave a throaty chuckle. "If that's okay with you, *boss*."

The sarcastic mention of my authority released frustration from its chamber. I covered my face with my hands and groaned as she continued to eat her dinner. "Do you always have to eat so loudly?"

"Do you always have to sleep in your vomit? Where were you at work today? I'm tired of filling in for you, night after night, leading those stupid humans in trivial tasks they should know already. I hate answering phone calls and bussing tables, smiling fake smiles that mean nothing to me in return. I can't stand coming home to you on the floor, passed out with an empty bottle under your arm. *What's happened to you?*"

"Get out of my head."

"*Where have you gone?*" she probed, ignoring my request. "Where's the strong, powerful merman that used to ride the ocean's fiercest wave? The one who'd grab the angriest of the devil sharks and rip it to pieces with his own bare hands—where has he fled? And now . . . well, look at you! Wallowing in your own filth, drinking poison that renders men useless. Truly, Marcus, you've lost your place in this world!" Her countenance became disgusted as she looked over my prostrated form.

My eyes locked with hers for a brief moment before closing again in defeat. The last remains of my self-respect wanted to rebuttal her observation. The part of me that looked in the mirror and refused to believe what I beheld wanted to object. But I knew I couldn't. The tragedy to my unraveling was just as much a mystery to me as it was to Avangeline. I couldn't deny the fact that I had eroded away to a pathetic, incorrigible wretch. My problems reached far deeper than any logical answers were found. Hope for me wasn't something I could grasp. Nights were bleak and typical. And what went down smooth and twinkled red in the glass, bit like a venomous snake and stung the next morning.

"What a paradox you've become," she concluded, closing her empty take-out box. She kicked both boots to the hardwood floor and folded her long legs under herself. "You have everything a human could ever want, yet you refuse to enjoy any of it. Your looks, your money, your power—all squandered. Why, you should become some directionless waiter or underpaid busboy. Perhaps you need to submit to an authority that's given. And a little sense of direction can probably do you some good."

At that moment, I knew she was merely prodding for a reaction. My silence only incited her anger.

"Aren't you going to respond? Marcus? Marcus? *Don't you have anything to say about that?*"

"I told you to get out of my head. Besides, what do you want me to say? That I agree with you? Sure. I agree. I let things slip. But you don't understand what I'm dealing with." I wiped away the vomit that had dried to one cheek and slowly lifted to sit.

"Well, can you enlighten me please? I am, after all, your roommate."

I struggled to focus on her shadowed face, but the alcohol wasn't finished with its pillaging. I drew my knees to my chest and rested my heavy head between them. "You don't understand because you hate them."

"I hate who?"

"Humans. All of them. Young, old, wealthy, poor, prestigious, lowly—you hate them all. You wouldn't care if you woke up tomorrow morning and every one of them had vanished."

Her hollow snicker agreed.

"So, why would I share my heart's sorrow with you if you can't even grasp the basics of humanity? To you, a man is to be used as a tool to get what you need. Fredrick, Gregory, Richard, Lance . . . all tools."

As if on cue, the muffled ring of her cell phone sounded from her pocket. She smirked at the irony and looked away.

"Gregory provides your clothing. Fredrick lavishes you with jewelry. Richard bought all your expensive technical devices. And Lance . . . well, I don't even know what Lance contributes."

"He's buying me a condominium this fall."

"See what I mean?" I spread my hands in her direction. "They all have money that you're taking—lives that you're ruining. Don't you feel any pity for those fools?"

"Why should I?" she snapped, uncrossing her legs. "What's wrong with me acquiring what I need? It's their choice how they spend their money, not mine. I'm not forcing anyone to give me anything."

"You're not forcing anyone, you're misleading them."

"Oh, stop it, Marcus! You and your silly opinions. They matter very little. Besides, what do my relationships have to do with your insufferable woes?"

The room fell quiet as I contemplated her question. If not for Avangeline, I would've never met Gwendolyn. She, in turn, would've never lost interest in Ryan, who gave his life to free Avangeline. Gwendolyn wouldn't have neglected his murder, which ultimately led to the damnation of her soul. Consequently, her deliverance as a mermaid required the entrapment of another human. If not for Avangeline, I would be dealing with the blood of my own victim. Not the melding of three.

Her cell phone beeped again.

"Do you have to get that? I'm merely trying to prove a point."

"Well, your point doesn't make any sense," she dismissed. She rose from her seat and walked to the window. The furrows in her forehead softened as she watched the steady stream of traffic travel down GlenPoint Strip. Car lights played with shadows across her face, changing it from severe and evil to breathtakingly beautiful.

"Do you ever dream of the future?" she whispered, barely audible from across the room. Her chest filled deep with a breath of air and then released. "Do you ever survey this land and ask yourself if there's something more out there? When you see your potential and all that you possess, do you ever wonder if you've reached your limit to becoming something great?"

I smoothed back the hair that fell before my face and held it with my hands. "What do you mean by great?"

"Well, take that man for instance. How did he become so powerful?"

I squinted in her pointed finger's direction to a large glowing billboard. A handsome man sat draped by two women in an advertisement for an expensive watch. I looked back at her and shrugged. "That man isn't powerful. He's a model."

"Yes, I know that," she hissed, sounding slightly embarrassed. "But how did he get there? How did he achieve such status? His face is admired by the whole city. He's able to communicate without needing to say a word. And the citizens of GlenPoint are listening."

I stifled a laugh for fear of the headache it would produce. Avangeline had learned a lot in the six months of living on land. She obviously hadn't learned enough.

"Advertisements don't communicate anything of importance. It's an easy way for companies to make money. That person doesn't have any clout or devout followers. He's just a good-looking man selling a watch."

She gave a sinister chuckle as she turned from her position in the window. Her full, heart-shaped mouth opened to a smile while she relished some unspoken thought.

I frowned at her naivety. "I'm not sure I see your point."

"Humans look to each other for guidance. Their lives are so impressionable that they will psychologically follow with the slightest of persuasion. Most of them, from what I've noticed, do so willingly. It's like they crave for someone to give them direction. I see it all the time at La Mer. I tell this one 'come' and they come. I tell the other 'go' and they go."

"Yes, of course. You're using your common influence. Your animal senses changed for human purpose once you received your legs."

"No. I'm not talking about common influence. That only controls people's movements. I'm talking about controlling the thoughts of the heart. The inner core of who a person really is."

"You can't touch that, Avangeline. No one can."

"Can't I? Well, don't be too sure. That part of man is always changing. It's a revolving door to suggestions and application. And there's no guard watching for visitors. I can easily slip in and develop an opinion. And in the process of developing an opinion, I can tear down what was previously thought to be truth and replace it with my own. We can use this ability for our advantage."

I ignored the threat of a splitting headache and gave a hearty laugh. It was baffling to me that a mere second ago I was voicing my distaste for her exploitation of men—she now speaks of capitalizing on something even greater.

"Our power doesn't have to end here," she said, scowling that I laughed. "You've chosen to settle for a small, crowded shoreline and the stuffy, painted walls of La Mer. I invite you to partake in something far larger. A life full of wealth, fame, and power . . ." Her eyes narrowed on her spoken words as if she were savoring the flavors of a delicate wine. She turned from the glow of the window and crossed the room to where I sat. The hardwood creaked beneath the pressure of her knees as she knelt to the floor to sit.

"Avangeline, I—."

"*Come with me,*" she whispered, reaching deep within my mind. "*Just you and me. Let's explore this world together. Cast off this bondage that has robbed you of all joy and drink deep from the waters of lust and pride. Set your mind on all that you want and receive all its benefits! For, truly, nothing we desire can be withheld from us.*"

I held her stare in growing pity and slowly shook my head. She didn't believe what she was saying. Her animalistic nature took her to depraved depths, yet there was one thing she knew she never could obtain.

Me.

Despite the droves of men that grappled at her door, her heart remained fixed on the one who couldn't love. Their eyes were deceived by her flawless visage, but I couldn't look past her blemished demeanor. The more I denied her romantic advances, the more I fed the flames of passion.

"Avangeline, listen. You can't think like a mermaid anymore. Your life changed once you received your legs. When we lived in the water, we did what we pleased. There weren't any laws or morale because there wasn't any accountability for our actions. We defended our territory and killed who we chose because we knew no other way. But the manner of man is not so. They're exceptionally fragile beings. They coexist with a level of respect. We can't push our way into their lives and use them for our pleasure. If anything, we should have as little communication with them as possible."

I swallowed the lump that formed in my throat and looked the other way. Gwendolyn's face surfaced, lifted in great pride, as she boldly attempted her murder. Her once rich and beautiful soul had been stripped by the immorality of its environment and was relishing in vile passions. An unexpected reunion on GlenPoint's shore would haunt me to my grave.

Avangeline's eyes narrowed as my lower lip began to tremble. She grasped a fistful of my thoughts and pulled apart their fabric.

"Is that what this is all about? That traitor? That bottom-dwelling scum that delivered her fiancé to his death? She's the reason you can't pick your head up off the ground?!"

I gave no response.

She cursed under her breath and rose to her feet. She marched to the corner of the room and turned on the lamp. My eyes squinted from the flood of light as she activated the recess lighting and the brass chandelier overhead. She walked in the direction of the kitchen and stopped. "Get up! Scrape yourself up off that ground and act like your kind! I'm not going to sit in the shadows to pacify your withdrawals." She looked at me in utter abhorrence and slowly paced the floor. The air in the room felt thick with wrath. "I've covered for you at work. I've paid your rent. I've dragged your lifeless body to bed while you reveled in your shame. And all you can think about is that human? How dare you allow me to care?"

I opened my mouth to rebuttal her comment, but then closed it. The possibility of convincing her that I didn't lead her on was hopeless.

"So, do you think she's pining away for your affection? Do you think she wishes for your love while she remembers her life on land? Her family, her friends, her dead fiancé—do you think she includes you in those losses? Or are you the reason she's so unfortunate? Don't think so highly of yourself, Marcus. Your relationship with her is the reason she's accursed. How foolish of you to invite her to witness Ryan's infidelity. Did you really think she would walk away from that unscathed? Was there not a small part of your being that feared she still loved him? Perhaps, be it slight, a chance that she would respond unfavorably to his death?"

She slipped behind the bar and grabbed her purse from the counter. She reappeared with a sneer. "She did nothing when his lips touched mine. Nothing. He gave me his soul like the imbecile that he was, and she just stood there and watched it happen. No intervention. No tears. No remorse. Just the silent approval of a shameless traitor. And the judgement of her transformation was the result. I guess you didn't see that coming, did you?"

She laughed in cruel satisfaction and headed for the door. Her hand rested on the knob for a thoughtful moment before she turned from her departure and smiled. "I actually feel very sorry for you. It's your face she'll see when she kisses her victim."

I unbuttoned my shirt because of the increase in temperature and stripped my tank top to the floor. The headache that lurked in the recesses of sobriety had finally made its appearance. And Avangeline's shrill voice wasn't helping either. I glared at her looming form in expectation of her exit. Her body stood stiff, hands clenched in tight fists, visibly furious at my indifference. Her black eyes were wide as they sought desperately for mine. I pushed past her ruffled appearance and looked deep into her heart.

She was planning her revenge.

Without saying another word, she gave our conversation a final nod and walked out the door.

Although Avangeline's parting was an invited relief, her words had overstayed their welcome. The statement that I was pinning away for Gwendolyn's love evoked a measure of insecurity. To think that a romantic relationship could destroy my well-being was nothing short of discouraging. It wasn't like there was a shortage of women to not cultivate love with another. But the fact remained that Gwendolyn was my first. She was my first real embrace. She was my first real kiss. She was the first person to show me what an upright spirit looked like. Honesty, faithfulness, humility—such concepts were so foreign amongst my kind. It was as if I had stumbled upon a god. It was such a shame that she ultimately fell from grace.

I ran my hand through my sweaty hair and slowly stood to my feet. The room took a nauseating spin as I stumbled past the armchair in the direction of the light switch. The darkness gave instant relief, fueling my shaky steps toward the lamp. Avangeline's menacing face appeared as the shadows of the night slowly enveloped my apartment. She was wrong in her assumption of my calamity. I wasn't grieving over the loss of Gwendolyn's relationship. I was grieving over the loss of her soul.

Chapter Ten

"*Gwendolyn! Hurry! Wake up!*" Sabrina screamed. "*Help me! Quick! She's getting away!*"

"*Who's getting away?*" I asked, roused from my sleep. I rubbed my eyes with groggy reluctance and parted the smooth pleats of kelp that served as my cover. A school of feeding mackerel scattered in a flash of silver and blue. The shadow of a floating sea turtle passed, and a cloud of bright pink krill swirled in the sunlight. Although the ocean's water was alive with the morning, Sabrina was nowhere to be found. Only a thin stream of bubbles stirred by her wake was visible in a ray of sun.

I reached my arms high above my head and stretched the muscles that ached in my back. Following Sabrina around on some witch-hunt was one of the last things I wanted to do. My body was sore from holding the surfboard all day, and I didn't get a great night's sleep. Not to mention the annoying task of taking orders from a mermaid who was equal to myself. I was tired of her persistent authority. In the beginning of our relationship, her direction in my life was welcomed—needed almost. But lately she pushed her dominance too far. She decided when she used the board and where we would surface. At times I wondered if I would be more successful if she wasn't calling the shots. I questioned if it was her goal—to keep me from becoming human. I was paranoid in our relationship, and I wanted to live alone.

I watched as a current of water swept through her effervescent path and dissolved it completely. Sabrina never asked me to catch someone before. Come to think of it, I couldn't think of who she would encounter that would pose such a challenge to catch. Humans didn't stand a chance escaping with their inefficient air-tanks and rubber flippers. She would've killed them in seconds and said nothing about it. But another mermaid entering our territory made perfect sense. It explained the speed of her passing and the urgency in her voice. The frustrating request that stole my tranquility suddenly became apparent. Sabrina was defending our area from an intruder of similar kind. If there was any temptation to return to my slumber, it vanished completely with a surge of adrenaline. I burst through the kelp that held me in paralysis and followed her elusive path.

"Who's getting away? Sabrina? Where are you?"

Fish. Coral. Rocks. Sand. Objects passed by in a blur as I sped through the obstacles of the ocean. Using common influence for communication and the effervescent wisp of a rapidly vanishing trail, I searched high and low for my acquaintance and the trespasser. I swam across a meadow of bright green seagrass and through a knobby structure of populated coral. Several large parrotfish dipped and swayed as they clustered lazily in an oblong formation. I flapped my tail hard against a swell of water and pushed the clumsy creatures out of my way. I needed to find our visitor, and I was running out of time. Another mermaid in our area was nothing more than competition. She needed to be captured immediately and escorted to her own territory. A strong threat of repercussion should keep her from wandering. The gods only knew I would keep true to my word.

"Sabrina? Where are you?"

I followed the tiny bubbles that rose high toward the ocean's glassy surface. They twinkled around a cluster of seaweed and down a craggy slope of basalt. Effervesce filled a long trench that was etched in the darkness. The crack widened to a plain and stretched on for what felt like miles. I dodged the hanging tentacles of a jellyfish and grazed my belly against the ocean's sandy floor. Pillow-soft sediment clouded with dust.

"I can't see you."

The more I swam and sought for her whereabouts, the more I became enraged with her absence. I kept my arms close to my sides to streamline my body for more speed.

"Sabrina!"

I strained to hear a response, but received none. The water became cool and thick. Shadows lengthened and became one. Unfamiliar species of life emerged that never appeared in my territory. I widened my eyes to receive more light and took in my foreign surroundings. I was in a different zone of the ocean. The bright blue waters I knew since my transformation had evolved to a place that was filled with darkness, obscurity, and possible threat. I cursed at the sight of a wide-mouthed eel and immediately came to a stop. I didn't know where I was.

"Curse you, Sabrina! You've gotten on my last nerve."

I looked at my hands that were clenched into fists and shook my head in discouragement. I couldn't believe my lack of judgement. I mindlessly obeyed her command without any hesitation and had nothing to show for it but a racing heart and lack of sleep. How dull of me to think I could use bubbles to locate her whereabouts. Sabrina's trail probably went cold the second I woke up.

A pale striped octopus slithered to a sea star and quickly closed around its appendages. I watched the ravenous mollusk pulse and quiver until my vision began to distort. The more I considered the last twenty minutes of my fruitless pursuit, the more I became resolved in my decision. I couldn't live with Sabrina any more than I could live with an intruder.

"You know what?!" I yelled, more to myself than to her. *"I'm done! I'm not living with you anymore. You've been dragging me down from the start. I'll surface when I want, where I want. You always—"*

A piercing scream sent a shiver down my spine.

The putrefying taste of blood and vomit instantly filled my mouth. I gagged on the acidic, stomach-churning emotion and wildly scanned the ocean for movement.

"Sabrina? Is that you? . . ." My voice trailed to silence as I took in every detail. Little could be seen in the shadowed, still world. A handful of chrome lantern fish suspended like stars in their black stretch of water. The flicker of light from a jellyfish

set off another a few yards away. The octopus that captured the unfortunate sea star slithered to a crevasse and pulled off its arm.

"Sabrina?"

"Quick! She's coming your way!"

"Where?"

I stiffened in expectation and looked up to see the faint silhouette of two fanning tails swimming toward the surface. I took off with instinctual force and followed their direction.

"Stop! Please! I didn't do anything wrong!" A high-pitched voice begged in the darkness.

Using both hands, I pulled at the water to propel my body forward and flapped my tail hard with determination. Every nerve ending stung with the expectation of her capture. The gradation of water transitioned from cobalt to turquoise, and the intertwined bodies of two fighting mermaids came into view. Sabrina yelled a curse, followed by a blood-curdling scream, and the water around them clouded to dark red.

"Stop fighting me, you idiot! I've already won. Gwendolyn, will you come over here and give me a hand with her?"

The intruder pulled away from Sabrina's clutch of her hair, but was immediately seized by her tail. The two bodies thrashed violently about in a tangle of fish and human. Another cry sounded through my head, and their area darkened with blood.

I snuck up behind the unsuspecting trespasser and grabbed her by her wrist. She shrieked in terror and spun around. My eyes met with hers, and I almost dropped her arm.

She was young.

The beautiful face that was etched with horror was too young to be a threat. Her wide eyes pleaded with mine before darting back to Sabrina's.

"Please don't hurt me! Please! I didn't do anything wrong."

"You let us be the judge of that. Grab her around her neck, Gwendolyn." Sabrina clutched her tail that flapped and swayed and gave it a hard twist. A deafening shriek filled my ears.

I grasped the writhing mermaid by her upper arm and pinned it behind her back. She threw her head back and hit my bottom lip. My mouth exploded with excruciating pain. I pushed away her hair that clouded my vision and slung my arm around her neck.

"Please, I promise you. I wasn't trespassing. I was in my own territory. You have to believe me."

"I don't have to do anything," Sabrina sneered. *"I told you to be quiet. You talk when we ask you to."* She looked at me and smirked. *"You can't believe anything this bottom-dweller has to say. She's a mermaid. She's been uttering lies since the day she was born."* She gave her tail another crank.

"Where's your territory?" I asked, tightening my arm against her movement.

"It's that way," she sobbed, pointing her finger. *"Where the fishing boats dock. Where the humans buy and sell."*

"GlenPoint Pier?" I glanced at Sabrina and raised an eyebrow. The pier was one of the most prized territories in all of GlenPoint. Droves of people gathered to the location simply because it was a tourist attraction. It wouldn't take a mermaid long to acquire legs by odds of sheer numbers. She was a fool to wander anywhere else.

"Yes. That's what it's called. I was asleep when your friend woke me up. She grabbed me by my hair and chased me here. Please! You have to believe—"

"Enough!" Sabrina's face twisted in fury. Her large, commanding eyes glazed to pitch black. *"I don't know why we're wasting our time talking to this deplorable little wretch. We should just finish her off and be done with her."*

The mermaid resisted again.

"What's your name?" I asked, pulling away from her thrashing head.

"Danielle. Please—"

"What's the real reason you're here, Danielle? You know you shouldn't wander out of your territory. What's wrong with your own?"

"Nothing! Nothing's wrong with my territory. Please, believe what I'm saying. Your friend, she . . . she—"

"Why are you still talking to her?" Sabrina's brow furrowed. *"What more is there to learn? She's a mermaid, and she's competition. Any sympathy shown is a waste of time. I'm beginning to question your good judgement."*

"Are you saying you never wandered off?" I inquired, ignoring Sabrina's objection. *"The pier is very close. Is it possible you lost track of where you were going and ended up here by mistake?"*

"No. I speak the truth. Your friend . . . she woke me up and chased me here. She was the one who—"

"Kill her!" Sabrina pulled off a piece of Danielle's fin, and the mermaid screamed. I sputtered on the blood that rushed in my mouth. *"By the gods, Gwendolyn, kill her! Kill her now!"*

"Please!" Danielle cried. *"Believe me! You have to believe me!"*

"What are you waiting for? Kill her!"

"But I didn't do anything wrong—"

"Kill her!"

"Please!"

Sabrina cursed, and Danielle resisted in a desperate effort to escape. She threw her head back and slammed my injured lip. My mouth throbbed in agonizing pain.

"Kill her!"

I firmly grasped the sides of the mermaid's head and gave it a hard twist. The breaking of a bone could be felt. Cords that held her neck upright were loosened, and her head slumped to one side. Her body that kicked and thrashed beneath my grasp, softened to flaccid and slowly stopped moving. I looked at the mermaid that floated before me and lowered my hands to my sides.

"Well, it's about time! Nice work. If I had to hear that whiny voice again, I think I would've died. You have to admit she was very annoying. Perhaps the most obnoxious I've come across in a while. No thanks to you for asking so many questions. There's really no point in conversing with her, you know. She'll just repeat the same story." Sabrina smoothed back her hair that billowed around her face and frowned. *"What's wrong?"*

"I . . . I . . ."

"You don't feel bad for killing her, do you? Why? She could ensnare your victim tomorrow. It's one less competitor to worry about. Besides, didn't you hear where her territory is? GlenPoint Pier! Isn't that great? We have twice the amount of water to cover now. You can thank me for that when you're finished brooding."

"Why should I thank you?" I asked, finally finding my voice. My vision followed the dead body that slowly sank to the sand. Danielle crumpled to the ocean's floor like an old, discarded t-shirt. *"I was the one who killed her."*

"Yes, but I was the one who chased her to you. You were only helping me out. I would've done the job myself if she wasn't so fast." She drew close to the mermaid and began to look her over. Her face lit with excitement, and she yanked off a thin shell necklace. *"I didn't expect for her to react with such quick reflexes. I just barely touched her hair, and she woke up swimming."*

"What?" My head whipped in her direction. I felt my face grow numb. *"She didn't trespass in our territory? She was telling the truth?"*

Sabrina lowered her prize and rolled her eyes. *"Of course she was telling the truth. I've been planning to kill her for weeks. Didn't you hear where her territory is?"*

A current of water swept through our location and the hair that covered Danielle's face swept to one side. Her expression was frozen in terror. Her eyes, wide with desperation, stared in my direction. I gave a hard swallow and looked the other way.

"Why didn't you tell me you were planning to kill her?"

"Why should I? You do things you don't tell me."

A crab scuttled to a nearby rock and disappeared within a crevasse. Every time I blinked, I saw her face.

"I questioned her, and you never said anything. You made me look like a fool, Sabrina."

"What difference does that make now? She's dead, isn't she? We have a new territory, don't we? Why spoil a great morning by perseverating on such trivial matters?" She made a sweeping motion with her hands as if to dismiss my concerns. *"Come, let's not talk about her anymore. I'm sure you're as famished as I am. I don't know about you, but that chase sure worked up an appetite."*

119

I grimaced at the thought of food and closed my eyes in repulsion. How could I put something in my mouth when I could still taste her blood? I was disgusted with Sabrina's cavalier attitude toward death. I was disgusted with myself. The dredges of my heart proved more debased than anything I ever imagined. If I could only get her face out of my head.

"Well? Are you going to put your differences aside and come join me, Gwendolyn? Gwendolyn?"

I suppressed the image that would haunt me to my grave and slowly opened my eyes. I screamed in horror and recoiled. Sabrina lifted from Danielle's waist and smiled in complete indifference. A small maroon cloud gathered around her mouth.

"Cursed hell, Sabrina, you're eating her?!"

I clasped my hand over my mouth and gagged as she grasped the side of the mermaid's tail and took a large bite. The hole immediately filled with blood.

"Of course I'm eating her," she mumbled, swallowing a mouthful. *"We have to destroy the evidence. At least half of her, anyways. If her body rises to the surface, we'll be in danger of being exposed. After we strip off her flesh and break apart her bones, we can scatter her remains across the sand, and she'll never be found."*

I covered my mouth with my hand and choked as the carnage continued to unfold. I had seen a lot of things in the six months of living with Sabrina. Her soulless lifestyle pushed boundaries beyond that which was conceivable. At times I found myself participating in those boundaries—even enjoying them. But this time she was taking things too far. It was a line I couldn't cross.

"Stop eating her." My voice was weak, but unmistakably certain. It cut through the moment like a knife.

"What?"

"Leave her alone."

"Why?"

"I can't watch you do this. There has to be another way to get rid of her. Eating her just seems . . . wrong."

"Wrong? What's so wrong about me eating my breakfast? I'm hungry. I worked hard to get this catch. Besides, she doesn't seem to mind." She playfully pushed the mermaid's arm and the body floated in my direction.

"Leave her alone. That isn't funny."

"What's the matter with you today? Why do you care for such insignificant things? You're the one who killed her. It doesn't make any sense. She was your victim."

"I know it doesn't make sense. I don't understand any of it myself. I just don't think we need to eat her, that's all. There has to be another way."

A muscle in her jaw pulled. "Your request is going to cost me my meal." She looked down at Danielle and then back up at me. "Well, what if I don't oblige? What if my hunger gets the best of me? Are you going to do something about that?" Her eyes narrowed on mine, and she smiled. In direct defiance, she opened her mouth to bare her teeth and lowered her head to the girl's torso. Her lips grazed her scales as if to tempt me to respond before slowly sinking in.

The frayed strings that held my composure together unraveled. All repulsion, all remorse, all questions as to how I found myself in the midst of such dissipation, vanished. The components that tortured the existence of my psyche were immediately replaced with one all-consuming emotion.

Wrath.

I conjured the fury that throbbed within my veins and pushed her hard with my mind. She ripped from Danielle's body and slammed hard against a nearby rock.

"Why, you little wretch!" She quickly lifted to swim in my direction, but I stopped her from proceeding. Her arms and tail fought madly in vain as an invisible force held her firmly in place. She pushed against the rock to gain better momentum, but her body refused to swim toward me.

"I told you to leave her alone, Sabrina. There has to be another way. I'm not going to beg for you to respect my wishes."

Her head twisted in my direction. She growled a torrent of obscenities. *"What an idiot you turned out to be! Defending the cause of some dead bottom-dweller. Is she worth you losing your safety? What are you going to do if she surfaces? Do you think humans won't tear this ocean apart in search of more of her kind? Do you think you will escape their curiosity? You're a fool to think otherwise. A bloody fool!"*

I looked down at the mermaid that lay mangled in the sand and shrugged my shoulders with indifference. There had to be another way. *"I'll find a way to get rid of her. There are plenty of ways to dispose of a body without having to eat it. But that really isn't your concern anymore, is it? I suggest you better find a different territory at this point, Sabrina. I don't think it's working out between us."*

Her face contorted in an effort to scream, but not a sound escaped. She longed to tear me from limb to limb and drink my blood to satisfy her revenge. Murder was her desire, and it was within her grasp, but she was powerless to touch a hair. No longer did our common influence weigh in her favor. As I silently obeyed and swam in her shadow, I grew strong enough to take total control. I just never knew it. An opportunity never arose for me to test my strength. A battle of flesh proved more than a territory conquered. Sabrina needed to give up complete dominance if she dwelled within my vicinity. It was a position she wasn't willing to take.

Her mouth drew a forced smile. *"If you think I want to live with you, you're wrong. It takes a great deal of effort to put up with your simple-minded instincts. You're more of a hindrance than anything."* She looked down at Danielle and shook her head with a snicker. *"You better get rid of her. I tell you the truth, if you don't do something with that body you'll be sorry. And don't expect for me to care. I'll have my legs by then."* She grinned at my expression and looked off toward the distance. Her eyes narrowed on a pod of passing dolphins. *"The pier is my territory now. I took it fair and square. Release your control, and I'll be on my way. We have nothing more to talk about."*

I pulled back my common influence with a measure of hesitancy and braced for her to tear my arms out of their sockets. But she hardly looked in my direction. She squared off her shoulders with her head held high and swam in the pier's direction. She paused before entering a forest of kelp and turned around.

"I'm really glad I'm leaving. This shore has been nothing but desolate these last few months. Besides, my victim has been surfing at the pier lately . . . so, this works perfectly for me. He asked if I could meet him there for our next date. Before I take his soul, I'll give him your regards."

"What?"

"Don't pretend you don't know who I'm talking about. Come on, friend, take a guess. No thoughts? Does the name

Joey Monroe bring any recollection? You know, your fiancé's best friend? I'm sure you made some great memories together. Joey was close to Ryan because he thought so much of him. Before you murdered him, that is."

I resisted the temptation to look away and stared at her straight in the eyes. She read my thoughts the whole time we lived together. The violation of my privacy was like a slap across my face.

She flashed a heartless smile and disappeared in the shadows.

I looked down at the mermaid whose life had been cut short and drew close to her marred body. A handful of small fish had already begun to feed on her torn flesh. It wouldn't take long for her living environment to decompose her remains.

I quickly swam to a pile of rocks and began the laborious task of covering her from head to tail. With each stone I placed, I felt remorse's sharp blade pierce deep within my heart. There seemed to be no redemption for a soulless creature such as myself. I was thankful for my aquatic world that wouldn't allow for tears.

***

A powerful storm struck the shores of GlenPoint, causing underwater currents to churn rocks and sand. The body of a dead mermaid floated to the surface.

Chapter Eleven

I threw my empty bottle in a nearby trashcan and stumbled down the dimly lit sidewalk. Although the evening's darkness had fallen upon the city, it couldn't hide my plight. To any innocent bystander I was a drunk, foolish man in need of a good shower. And they were right to pass judgement. Tonight I wasn't greeted with friendly smiles or pleasant first impressions. I was lucky if people didn't clutch their handbags and gasp as I walked in their path.

I tripped over a crack in the pavement and staggered to one knee. Several families returning to their cars laughed and talked joyously as they walked in my direction. I remained knelt to the ground and pretended to tie my shoe. I dare not attempt to stand lest I fall on my face and garner pity. A little girl who was barefoot and still wearing a bathing suit toddled past me toward a broken bottle that was strewn across the sidewalk. Her father called her name and broke from the group to save her. He scooped her up in his arms and gave her a kiss on the cheek.

I averted my eyes from their show of affection and continued to fiddle with my shoe. A cold sweat broke out across my skin as the familiar feeling of nausea took over. I shut my eyes in dread and wished for the families to leave. Falling to the ground could be explained as a misstep on bad pavement, but vomiting in front of children was traumatizing at best.

Several car doors slammed, and engines roared in the distance. I lifted my head and grimaced as I assessed the disappearing crowd. The last remaining couples had left, and the parking lot was empty. The muscles in my abdomen knotted, and I pulled at my sweat-soaked collar. Their absence gave me a comfortability to do my business with decency. I took in a gargled breath and emptied my stomach on the pavement.

Just get there.

I spit the remnant of vomit in my mouth and took a dizzy stand. The world around me spun as I staggered through the vacant parking lot and crossed onto the beach's sand. The roaring surf collided with the shore, spreading a sheet of shadowed water across my path. My foot got caught in a puddle of foam, and I fell to my back with a slam. I didn't get as far as I hoped, but the tide would eventually rise.

Cover me.

I was finished. I had enough. My life wasn't worth living. I was written in a tragedy that was wrought with bloodshed, and I was the murderer on trial. Sure, my life showed potential from time to time. Money was spent on the next great thing. Women were more beautiful than their predecessors. Alcoholic drinks flowed like water. But the outcome was always the same. I'd wake up to a morning that offered no mercy and fall asleep in a bed that offered no rest. There had to be an end to my calamity. The ocean would finish it all tonight.

A wave tumbled to the shore, and water spread across my legs. The cold splash against my skin caused my breath to catch in my throat.

My eyes took in a full moon and slowly filled with tears. I remembered my mother. Her soft, gentle demeanor was a rarity amongst my kind. She trained me in the ways of entrapping and loved me the best way she knew how. But her love for the land was always stronger. The night I awoke and reached for her comfort, I knew she had gone. Her arms would no longer hold me in the darkness. As a young, naive boy, I lingered near the shore and waited for her to return. Her abandonment was as predestined as the night I would take my life.

Another wave spilled, and water covered my waist. Foam lingered like a wisp of smoke and dissipated in the darkness.

Love was meaningless. It was something I could never obtain. Out of the many women who entered my apartment, there was only one who loved me unequivocally—my victim. Emma was so willing to give her heart away. With all the right words, I was able to convince her that she was the one for me. Perhaps I spoke the things I always wanted to hear. Out of the void in my life, she was filled to the brim. It took little effort to take her soul with a kiss. But it was within that moment when she beat against my chest that I knew I made a grave mistake. My transformation gave me a soul, and it ached with regret. It was a feeling I wasn't prepared for. If only there was a way to take it all back.

Another wave boomed and spilled. I gasped as the water covered my chest and reached to the bottom of my neck. I opened my eyes and found the moon was totally covered by clouds. A bright, twinkling star peeked through the spreading haze.

So was Gwendolyn when she entered my life! She was so different from everyone else I knew. Sure, she was physically attractive, but it was her upright spirit that enraptured my heart. I remembered the day when we first met, and she fought so hard to stay faithful to her fiancé. Her firm resolve to reject my advances was something I never experienced. I appeared in her life to distract her from her relationship, only I was the one who was distracted.

A break in the haze allowed for the moon to illuminate the shore. A large wave stretched across the sand and touched the bottom of my chin.

I could still see her face. Her cheeks flushed pink with nerves. Her hands twisted in her lap. What was supposed to be an exciting first date at my club became a sweaty attempt at starting our relationship with honesty. She was so determined to tell me about her engagement to Ryan. Most people would've prevented such details from spoiling the moment, but she insisted on remaining true to her convictions. Her profound expression of integrity had me breathless across the table.

The ocean thundered and crashed. A wave shot across the sand and spread over my head. For a terrifying moment, I began to suffocate underwater as my mind and heart began to race. My body desired to pull up from the current, but a firm resolve told me to remain still. Water burned within my eyes and flooded up my nose. I lifted my hands in total surrender and readied my lungs to aspirate the water. But the wave that churned forcefully above my head leveled across the shore and lowered from my face. I spit out a mouthful of salty grit and struggled to take a breath.

Another image of Gwendolyn surfaced. Her hollow, insensitive eyes narrowed as they raked me up and down for answers. She kissed me with hopes of becoming a human and was confused why I didn't die. Her disappointment at my survival was unexpected. It cut deep. No longer was she a gentle, sweet spirit who showed me true morality, but a cold, bloodthirsty animal who relied on deception to survive. It was a shame I made a promise to help her that night on the shore—a promise I couldn't keep.

Another wave struck and rose above my head. My heart picked up speed.

"You can talk to me," I whispered, tucking a strand of Gwendolyn's hair behind her ear. I cupped her face with both my hands and smiled.

Water rushed into my mouth and poured down the back of my throat.

"I will always be here for you. We'll figure this thing out. If there's another way to transform you into a human, I promise I'll find out what it is. Just don't give up. Don't give up hope."

My heart pounded in my ears as my lungs squeezed painfully within my chest.

A little girl toddled to a broken bottle that was strewn across the sidewalk. Her father called her name and ran down the pavement to save her. He scooped her up in his arms and gave her a kiss on the cheek.

I pulled out of the wave that pummeled me to the ground and gasped wildly for air.

There was a way.

***

The murky shadow of a large gray mound slowly material-ized to a pile of smooth stones. I made my way through the forest of kelp and lowered to the ocean's crumbly floor. The location I visited so many times before had all at once thrust me like a tumultuous wave. No longer did my calendar stones remind me of Brandon's date to come, but of the gravesite of the mermaid I murdered in cold blood. My stomach twisted in knots at the thought of her crumpled body in the sand. I suppressed the image that tortured my existence and picked up a large rock.

One.

I turned it over in my hands and set it to the side. I grabbed another.

Two.

I placed it to the side and grasped another.

Three.

With every stone I touched, I felt the days weigh heavy.

Four.

A day of watching and waiting.

Five.

A day of remembering times past.

Six.

A day of wanting my old life back.

Seven.

A day of torments and regrets.

Eight.

I counted and transferred stones from one pile to another for what felt like hours. It seemed as though every time I picked one up another appeared in its place. I studied the large mound that grew at my side and tilted my head in confusion. The amount of rocks I had left over didn't make sense. If they coincided with the day I was supposed to meet with Brandon, there should be only a few left to count, not a huge pile. I struggled to remember the number I left off on and continued my calculation.

Fifteen.

I flung the stone to the side and seized another.

Sixteen.

And another.

Seventeen.

Eighteen.

My eyes were drawn to a large, jagged rock that protruded from the rest. I dug my fingers deep within its rough crevices and pulled with all my strength. The rock dislodged with a rush of water and several supporting stones fell to the ground. The mound slowly shifted as if suspended in time and broke apart. I looked down at the half-circle scattering and recoiled.

The body of Danielle lay decomposing in the sand.

Her skin, once creamy and flush with emotion, had turned almost completely gray. Her tail was no longer a thick, powerful muscle but a withered, kelp-like strip. I cleared away the sand that covered her face and looked around me in disbelief.

How could this be her gravesite?

Why didn't I notice I was at the wrong pile? It didn't make any sense. I traveled to this location so many times that I knew it like the back of my hand. Surely, there would have been some sense of familiarity when I arrived. I shooed away several fish that were trying to feast on the dead mermaid as my mind groped for answers. Scenes from the day I killed her flashed before my eyes.

Sabrina smiled in complete defiance and threatened to take a bite out of the girl's waist. I channeled all the wrath that coursed through my veins and pushed her hard with common influence. She screamed as she flung through the water and slammed against a rock . . . over there. I realized she violated my mental privacy before she disappeared into a forest of kelp . . . over there.

I pulled off a small lemon shark that covered Danielle's arm and sent it on its way. Yes, there was no doubt about it. I was at the wrong location. I would have to bury her again, which was going to take time. The morning was far too spent to retrieve my board and wetsuit. I groaned with growing anger and waved away another fish.

But how could I be so mistaken?

My eyes wandered to the mangled lump of flesh that barely resembled her face. Her decomposing expression remained frozen in a perpetual state of horror. I winced and struggled to look away, but I couldn't stop staring. Her wide, cloudy eyes begged mine for something I couldn't give.

I tore my vision from our silent communication and focused on her arm. There was an object she was wearing that wasn't there when I buried her. I bit down on my lower lip as my heart began to pound. A shackle was attached to her wrist. The heavy metal cuff was connected to a chain that was buried beneath where she lay. I picked up the rusty restraint and gave it a hard tug. It wouldn't budge. Beneath the weighty suppression of sand and rock, the chain was adhered to something quite large. Whoever shackled Danielle to the ground went through great lengths to ensure she wouldn't move.

This was impossible.

No one knew of her location. I buried her alone, and I was certain no one saw me do it. And what would be the motive for keeping a dead mermaid restrained underwater? I scanned the distant forest of kelp, halfway expecting to find Sabrina laughing in the shadows. Her threats of curious humans probing the depths of the ocean all came flooding to remembrance. If anyone felt the need to do such an act, it would only make sense it was Sabrina. She wanted to make sure Danielle was never found—or perhaps she wanted to make sure she was. Revenge would be her desire.

The more I contemplated the disturbing predicament, the more I needed answers. I desperately grabbed two handfuls of sand and threw them over my head. Something told me the chain would be attached to the bigger picture. I reached beneath the cumbersome body and dug until my fingers throbbed. Sand billowed around my face, making the simple task of excavating near impossible. I blindly reached into the hollowed-out gravesite and rolled Danielle to one side. The clunky chain pulled with her arm and an attached object brushed against the tips of my fingers. I felt its length with both hands and drew a mental picture. I lifted out of the hole and screamed.

Another arm was shackled to the chain.

My vision pulsed in sync with my heartbeat. Sand continued to waft around the gravesite like a curtain drawn so no one could see. I smoothed back my hair with trembling hands and waited for the dust to settle. The hole and its remains slowly came into view. Another body lay in the sand. The form was that of a human, with long, narrow legs descending from their waist. They were much larger than Danielle—perhaps a male, judging from their build. My heart hammered in my ears as I waited to get a visual of their face. I leaned in close as the last puff of sand settled around the body.

I gasped and spun around to leave.

It was Ryan.

I flapped my tail hard to swim away, but something held my arm. I looked down at my wrist and cried out in terror. I was shackled to the chain.

I pulled out of my nightmare and looked toward the water's dark surface. Today was Brandon's date.

Chapter Twelve

He was old, but too young to die. His hand trembled slightly as he zipped up his jacket. He cleared his throat in an effort to speak and smiled with genuine appreciation. I looked at him through the corner of my eye and continued to focus on the road. His appearance was rough and weathered. His face was creased and thin. His mustache that was once mahogany in color had turned almost completely white. He was a mere shadow of what I remembered—a thin, frail old man with the weight of the world on his shoulders. Time and grief had certainly taken their toll.

"There's not a lot of traffic at this time in the morning," Mr. Hart commented. His voice caused me to jump in my seat.

"No, there really isn't," I stammered.

When I appeared on Gwendolyn's front doorstep, I knew I was taking a gamble. Mrs. Hart clung to her husband in horror as I sat in their living room, wet and covered with sand, and relayed the details they waited seven months to hear. Their daughter had transformed into a mermaid and was stranded out at sea. Only a few minor details were carefully omitted—the murder of Ryan and her curse for contributing to it. Some things were best left unsaid. Still, I knew I sounded like a drunk lunatic when I explained her tail in great detail. And maybe that was my only saving grace. No one in their right mind would show up at twelve o'clock in the morning with such a radical story to convey.

"Did you have a fun time at the beach tonight?" Mr. Hart looked over my clothes that were still covered with sand and chuckled good naturedly. I swept the grit from the sides of my pants and laughed along with him. The levity in the moment made my heart sink.

"I was taking a stroll by the water and accidently fell in. That's how I found out your daughter transformed."

His silence to my response made me shift with unease. Gwendolyn's parents handled my story with a surprising measure of grace. There were no snickers or threats to call the authorities—only the undying embers of reuniting with their long-lost daughter. Perhaps love blindly hoped for all things.

"Well, I'm very grateful you found her, Marcus. Mrs. Hart and I will go to the ends of the earth to see our daughter again. Let's just hope she's still at the shore."

"Yes. Let's hope so."

I made eye contact with him briefly and stopped at a red light. My fingers tapped out a rhythm on my steering wheel, and I dropped my hand in my lap. The suggested remedy I proposed didn't come without risks. Her redemption was prefaced with a solemn warning of death. Mr. Hart would leave his wife widowed while his daughter walked from the shore. It was a challenge he unflinchingly accepted. And, yet, there was a glimmer of hope to the foreboding act of heroism. There was a possibility of another way. When I was young, I heard a story of a victim's fate being pardoned with the giving of true love. The mermaid transformed into a human, and her victim never died. Although my mother never saw it happen, she said true love presented the perfect sacrifice. In contrast to lust which gives the soul carelessly, true love does so with intent.

"I found Gwendolyn at lifeguard station twelve. Thankfully, the parking lot gates are still open."

"Lifeguard station twelve? That's where she and Ryan were last seen."

I frowned at the mention of Ryan and parked under a glowing streetlamp. Mr. Hart could possibly share the dead fiancé's fate. It was an outcome I didn't want to take part in. As I sat uncomfortably in Gwendolyn's stuffy living room, I waited for her parents to discuss their future. Mrs. Hart wept softly as she whispered her concerns to her husband. He stroked her hair and reassured her that everything was going to be okay. I wiped the sweat that beaded at my brow and wished to bolt out the door. I really didn't think things over. By the time the alcohol left my system, it was too late for me to retract my story. Mr. Hart was already getting into my car.

He reached to open the door and took in a sharp breath. "Well, let's go see if she's still here. Did you tell her to wait for us?"

I rolled up my window and turned the car off. "No. I didn't have time. She was running out of air, so we couldn't talk for long. But she keeps her belongings in a cleft by the tide pools. Maybe we'll get lucky, and she'll come back for them."

"Belongings?'

I reached to the backseat and pulled out a bright purple backpack. Her parents were able to provide clothing and a towel in case her transformation was successful.

"She found someone's surfboard and wetsuit on the shore. I'm not sure what she uses them for. As I said, she was running out of air . . . so, we had to part ways. She told me she needed to get back to the water." I stepped out of the car and slung the pack over my shoulder.

Mr. Hart closed his door and walked to where I stood. He was a short man, standing a little taller than my chin. He adjusted his glasses to get a good look at my face and frowned at my expression. "Marcus, listen. I know you think you saw her. I don't doubt you're convinced. Mrs. Hart and I think we see her, too. All the time. At the grocery store. In the post office. I thought I saw her jogging down our street yesterday. We would give anything to see our baby daughter again. But we're losing hope. It's only our broken hearts that manifest that image." He looked toward the ocean and swallowed.

I scratched the back of my neck and waited for him to gather his composure. His chin quivered slightly, and he wiped his face with a tissue in his pocket. He turned back to face me, but his visage was stricken with agony. His eyes glistened in the moonlight. "Are you absolutely positive it was her? Is it possible you saw someone else that looked like her? Maybe she had Gwen's features? Maybe she shared the same name? Could it have been someone else that you saw, wearing a bathing suit that looked like a tail? I've seen those before, and they look very real—particularly in the dark. Is it possible that she was pretending to be a mermaid, and she was pulling your leg?" His wide eyes darted eagerly across my face.

"No. I'm positive it was her."

His mouth drew a thin line. He whispered something that sounded like a prayer and gave a weak smile. "I sure hope you're right. Let's go see if she's still here."

***

I looked down at my pile of calendar stones and counted them again to be sure.

"Fourteen, fifteen, sixteen, seventeen . . ."

If I calculated the days correctly, today was the first day of September. The long-awaited date with Brandon was finally here. Only, I wasn't very excited. The last few days have been an agonizing struggle with the two beings of my existence. The animal within me desired to take Brandon's soul and relish in her victories, but the human grieved over who I had become. I hated myself for killing Danielle. I hated myself for allowing Ryan to die. I hated myself for trying to kill Marcus. The guilt I felt was tearing me to pieces, yet I found myself counting the days with great relish. I wanted to love humans and embrace my new environment, yet every day before dawn I put on the wetsuit to entrap. My mind was corrupt. I couldn't trust it. It gave little room for choice. It was like I was ruled by some unseen force, relentless and unyielding, and every time I reflected on the decisions I was making, I realized my life was not in my control.

I needed help.

My hand closed around a crab that was stuck between two rocks, and I set him on the sand. The little crustacean waved his claw with excitement as he scuttled across the ocean's rocky floor. Lately, I found myself occupied with tasks to benefit the goodwill of others. I freed a dolphin that was trapped in an old fishing net. I collected trash in my territory and buried it in a cave at the surface. I even converted to a vegan diet and ate seagrass and kelp. I tried my best to balance the scales that weighed so heavily in my heart, but they always tipped to one side.

I restrained myself from seizing the crab as he disappeared behind a rock. My stomach growled from the morning's neglect, and I grabbed a handful of kelp. I reluctantly chewed on the rubbery plant and looked up to the ocean's shadowed surface. The morning had not yet come. If there was any chance to meet with Brandon, I needed to leave and get my surfboard and wetsuit. Our date could serve a different purpose. Yes, the temptation to take his soul would be present, but the thought of enjoying a human's company made my heart leap for joy. I could experience laughter again. I could share about my day and hear about his. I wouldn't tell him I was a mermaid, of course. We could talk about simple things like the changing weather, or his surfing abilities. I smiled at the thought of our last encounter and made a mental list of things to mention. Just the idea of having a conversation with someone other than myself soothed my troubled mind.

My eyes focused on an object that was buried in the sand, and I quickly dug it out. I inspected my findings by a ray of moonlight and turned it over in my hands. It was an old tennis shoe. I flinched at a thought of running in the grass and quickly acted to suppress it. With one hand I clutched the wretched shoe, with the other I made my way for the surface. I could bury my trash in the cave when I retrieved my wetsuit.

***

I swallowed the lump that was lodged within my throat and pointed to the sand dune in the distance. "Gwendolyn's just past that hill. The walk isn't very far or difficult to maneuver. Just try to be careful when we get close to the tide pools. They can be really slippery in the dark."

Mr. Hart assured me he would watch his steps and thanked me again for my efforts. I locked my car door even though I wanted to run and silently led him to the shore. I couldn't tell if he believed what I was saying or not. Accepting such a fairytale took faith beyond measure. My reputation was at stake, and I could be subject to the authorities, but that was the least of my concerns. I was becoming increasingly uncomfortable with leading a man to his death. I hardly knew this desperate father who followed me in the darkness. He seemed like a good enough person. It wasn't fair that he had to pay such a costly price for his daughter's freedom. I was furious with myself for putting him in such a predicament. He would become another victim to add to my list.

It would've been better for me to die on the shore.

My pace quickened to a stride as the horseshoe cluster of rocks came into view. I motioned for him to join me, and we crouched behind the algae-covered wall. I peered through the narrow crack and surveyed the shore on the other side. The shadows of the morning made things difficult to see. There was an endless stretch of creamy white sand and an ocean that refused to be stationary, but there wasn't a mermaid. I let out my breath in an angry hiss and slowly shook my head.

"Mr. Hart, I can't guarantee she'll be here tonight. The chances of her surfacing while we're watching are pretty slim. I hope I'm not wasting your time."

He pulled his head out from two rocks and adjusted his glasses. "You're not wasting my time, Marcus. You're giving me hope. Until tonight, Mrs. Hart and I feared the worst. I'll stay here all night if I have to."

I looked at my watch by the light of the moon and peered back through the crevice. Although it was the same time when I ran into her weeks ago, it would take nothing short of a miracle to see her again.

"Is there a reason why we're hiding here?" he called, scaling the side of the rock to get a better view. His foot slipped on the wet exterior, and he fell to the sand. "Shouldn't we wait for her at the water's edge? That way she'll see us and come to the surface."

I looked at the sheet of spreading foam and took a few steps back. Gwendolyn wouldn't surface if she saw humans were standing on the shore. The suggestion to do such a thing was incredibly tempting. Mr. Hart would return to home disappointed, but his life would be spared. He would live his days seeing mirages of his daughter, but his wife wouldn't be widowed. As I studied the father, who was covered in sand, I sighed deep within my soul. He was standing in a puddle that reached to his shins.

"No. If we stand at the shore we will most likely deter her from surfacing. She wouldn't be able to see who we are and would feel threatened by the presence of humans. I'm not only suggesting that we stay hidden, I'm asking for you to let me talk to her first when she surfaces. I think I need to prepare her for your arrival. If that's okay with you."

He turned around and frowned. "That's going to be hard for me to do. I've waited for a long time to see her." A wave rolled to where he stood and submerged him to his knees. The man appeared unaffected by his volatile environment. He gripped the rock for better stability and wedged himself deeper inside the crevice. "But if you think you need to clarify why I'm here, I'll let you talk to her first. And I don't mind hiding so she doesn't see us. Whatever it takes to save my baby girl." His voice barely carried above the thundering surf.

At that moment, I wanted to pull him from the rocks and drag him back to my car. I wanted to tell him it was a story fabricated in the mind of a despondent alcoholic. I wanted to yell obscenities and scare him from the shore. I had to do something to keep him from possibly giving his life.

"Marcus! Look! Look! I think I see someone! Look!"

"What?!" My blood ran cold in my veins. I spun around and nearly tripped over a piece of driftwood as I joined him at the rocks. I cleared away the kelp that blocked my vision and looked through the narrow crack.

The silhouette of a mermaid appeared on the shore.

Chapter Thirteen

I relaxed the muscles that were tense in my body and allowed for the powerful surf to suck me in its mount. The wave pulled back with a mighty swing and crashed upon the land. Foamy gray water spilled across the shore, allowing for my body to slide effortlessly in one smooth motion. My momentum came to a stop when I reached drier sand, and I lifted to a cobra-like stance. My eyes scanned quickly for any unseen visitors before eventually settling on the tumbling waves. No matter how many times I arrived at the surface, my heightened sense of awareness never lessened.

After taking a moment to examine the beach, and seeing no one was present, I smoothed back my hair that was plastered across my face and picked off the pebbles on my chest. An incoming wave rose to the middle of my torso, and my fins gripped the sand for more stability. The water quickly lowered as it spread across the sand in a sparkling blanket of ivory foam. I took another look at my vacant surroundings and quickly slithered my way to the cave.

As I approached the rocky cleft that appeared in the shadows, I grunted in growing discouragement. Driftwood. Lots and lots of driftwood barricaded the entrance. I often wondered if it would be easier for me to hide my belongings in a different location. The strenuous chore of clearing a path used precious air and energy. Not to mention, the longer it took for me to enter the cave, the more I risked being discovered. The only reason I continued to return was because no one found my possessions. If anything, the continual appearance of wood prevented people from entering. For as much as it was a hindrance to deal with day after day, it was a blessing I never took for granted. I looked down at the branches that were scattered like matchsticks and began to throw them to the side.

A night-traveling seagull squawked loudly overhead, and I lifted my waist in apprehension. My eyes darted to the horseshoe cluster of rocks, and I scanned them carefully for movement.

Someone was watching me.

I turned to the structure of lifeguard station twelve and noticed nothing out of the ordinary. The long expanse of sand that stretched across the horizon continued to remain vacant. I looked to the hill that erected in the distance and saw no one was there. The muscles in my stomach unclenched, and I picked up another piece of wood.

In just a few short hours I was going to meet with Brandon.

The long, empty days of watching and waiting were finally over. But this cold September morning as I cleared my path to my cave, I didn't feel as I had expected. There was an incredible sadness I didn't see coming. A sadness that pressed so heavy I could hardly breathe under its weight. There was no grandeur hope that fueled my deceptive efforts, only a harsh reality that was slowly setting in. I would always be condemned to a life of a mermaid. No matter how strong the temptation would be to take Brandon's soul, I couldn't commit murder again. I couldn't bear to have another body shackled to mine. Our meeting would have to end with a warning for him to never return.

I bent to the ground and rolled away a heavy log. I snaked a few feet forward and bent to the ground again. Time passed by in a blur as I absent-mindedly cleared the pathway of the cave. I straightened my posture to throw a piece of wood and craned my neck to get a good look at the parking lot.

I froze.

A black sports car was parked under a streetlamp. Gooseflesh ran down my arms, and my face broke out in a cold sweat. I threw the branch I was unknowingly squeezing and frantically slipped inside the cave.

My trembling hands fumbled in the darkness as I groped for my wetsuit and stretched the rubbery material over my head. I felt along the rocky wall and bent to the ground to retrieve my surfboard. If I could just get back to the water, I would look like a passionate surfer enjoying a late night swim. My pathway to the ocean was sure, but I had little time to lose. I tucked the board under my arm and exited the cave to leave. I turned around, and Marcus stepped out from the rocks.

"Hello, Gwendolyn." His smooth voice revealed little enthusiasm. His eyes darted from the surfboard under my arm to the wetsuit I was wearing.

My heart hammered in my chest.

This was it.

My opportunity to make things right had finally come. For weeks I had hoped to run into Marcus and apologize for the night I tried to take his life. My vicious actions plagued me like a debilitating pestilence and nothing took it away no matter how hard I tried. With every piece of trash I collected, with every animal I attempted to save, with every night I fell asleep hungry with a bellyful of seaweed and kelp; I yearned to rectify my decisions. The only way to clear my conscience was to talk to him myself.

"Marcus?" My eyes glanced to his and fell. I looked to the scattering of wood on the ground and swallowed. "I'm so glad to see you. I've been wanting to talk to you about something really important."

His eyebrow raised, and he crossed his arms across his chest. He scrutinized my face like I was a dirty dog he found on the shore. He didn't believe what I was saying.

"Oh? You've wanted to talk to me?"

"Yes. I've wanted to talk to you for a while now. I'm very sorry—" My voice wobbled, and I coughed. "I'm so sorry for how I treated you the other night."

His eyes held mine for a few seconds and narrowed. My face burned hot with embarrassment, but I didn't turn away. I couldn't. I had to make things right for him. I had to make things right for me.

"I know you don't believe what I'm saying. If you want, you don't have to stand so close. I'm not going to ask you for a kiss or anything. That's not what this is about." I paused to let him respond, but he said nothing. I pushed past my hurt feelings and continued. "I feel horrible for how I've treated you. I've thought about the night I kissed you so many times. I wish I can take it all back, but I can't. There's so many regrets I have." My lip trembled, and I bit it. "I don't know how I became who I am. I look at myself and all that I've done and wonder what happened to my life. I'm not making excuses for my behavior, but it feels like there's two people living inside me. One person doesn't care about what it takes to become a human. The other person—" I stopped and closed my eyes. A burning tear streamed down my cheek and ran into the corner of my mouth. "The other person is tormented with regret. I would give anything to change who I've become. I hate myself."

"I can tell you what happened to you."

I looked up from the sand. The tone of his voice didn't match his cold expression. His voice sounded sorrowful.

"You're not a human anymore. You're a mermaid. You're half animal. In every practical sense, you do have two people living inside you. For as long as you have a tail, you won't be yourself. There will always be a struggle between the person you want to be and who you really are. In your thoughts you desire to do what is right, but your heart deceives you to do otherwise. You're wicked and debased. You're a fallen creature . . . and that's okay. I brought someone here to save you."

"What?"

"I brought someone to save you. Do you remember when I promised I would find another way?"

My confused expression answered his question.

"The other night when you and I kissed, I promised I would find another way to transform you into a human."

He took in a deep breath and let it out loudly. He looked as though he wanted to cry. "I found another way."

"What? What are you talking about?"

He grasped both of my hands and gave them a gentle squeeze. His eyes softened as they locked with mine. "Gwendolyn Hart, I forgive you."

The grace was so unexpected it made me gasp. I held his glistening stare and blinked.

"Really?"

"Yes."

"You do?"

"Yes, I do."

"Oh, I don't know what to say. Thank you. Thank you so much. You don't know how badly I've wanted to hear you say that."

He didn't say anything in return. He smiled, but his face was afflicted with emotion. There was a visible anguish that didn't have an obvious cause.

"Marcus?"

"Yes?"

"Do you love me?"

He thought about my question for a moment, and his face darkened. He slowly shook his head. "No, I'm sorry. I don't. Why?"

"Because for the first time since I transformed, I can taste water. Gosh, I can taste water! It's the purest, sweetest water I've ever tasted!"

He flinched at my words and slowly released my hands. As he stepped to the rocks that surrounded us in the shadows, a silhouette of a man emerged.

It was my father.

***

Gwendolyn recoiled in shock. Her face, pale and stricken with confusion, contorted to a silent cry as her father stepped into view. The eager man didn't wait to be called. He shouted her name with a voice that carried above the waves and broke out in a full run. The two clung to each other in a show of affection I never saw before.

I had awakened.

For the first time in my life, I saw what love's truest form looked like. It didn't come with a showy display. It didn't have all the right words. It didn't have an ulterior motive. I would have hardly recognized anything out of the ordinary if I wasn't standing six feet away. I watched in awe-struck wonder as a father filled with gratitude and joy held his long-lost daughter for the first time in seven months. His embrace was loving and tender. She said something inaudible, and he wept in the crook of her neck. He never raised an eyebrow or gawked at her appearance. It was as if there was never a tail that descended from her waist. He simply embraced the malformed state his daughter was in and didn't question the rest. For as comfortable as the man was with the creature that wept in his arms, Gwendolyn didn't handle her differences so well. She spread her hands across her tail in a feeble attempt to hide her abnormality. Her father, noticing her efforts, shook his head with a smile and whispered something in her ear. She wiped her tear-stained face with the back of her hand, and they both sat on the sand.

I looked at the ocean that crashed in the distance and walked a few paces toward it. For as badly as I wanted to stop the inevitable, I knew it was no longer my place. And there was nothing I could do to prevent him from rescuing her anyways. Mr. Hart would give his life for his daughter and would have it no other way. He ceased to exist the moment I presented her need. And, in a strange turn of events that I didn't see coming, I was completely at peace with the decision he was making. I was certain he wouldn't lose his life. After seeing his selfless sacrifice and all that he bestowed, how could he? How could such a pure love not be enough?

"But I deserve this form! I can learn to embrace my new environment, and we can communicate from afar."

I froze. It was a miracle I could hear their conversation over the crashing waves. A small voice in my head told me to give them their privacy, but blatant curiosity got the best of me. I slowly inched in their direction and pretended to inspect a piece of driftwood with my shoe.

"No. The ocean isn't your best. You can't live like this anymore. You belong here on land."

"But I've changed, Dad. I'm not the daughter you remember anymore. I've done some horrible things . . . things even you can't forgive."

"My love for you can forgive anything."

"I doubt it. You don't know what I've done."

"Then you don't know my love. It reaches farther than you can imagine. It's existed from the moment you were born and will be here until the end. Nothing you can say or do will change my love for you."

Gwendolyn breathed with a shrill rasp and buried her face in her hands. Her body shook in a sob. "I've committed murder. I killed another mermaid without any motive or hesitation. What about that? Does that change things?"

I held my breath and leaned in close. The roaring of the ocean, a distant car horn, the very pulse that hammered in my head—all threatened to drown out their hushed conversation. But I needed to hear his answer. All my questions of mercy and grace and how far such concepts reached resided in the response of one frail, old man. I tilted my head in their direction and strained to listen.

"I still love you," he said simply. He cupped her face in his hands so he could look into her eyes. She tried to look to the ground, but he tilted her chin toward his face. "My love for you will never fail. It isn't something you've earned. It doesn't go away when you've done something wrong. My love for you will give everything I have."

Gwendolyn's big eyes filled with tears. She slid from her father's embrace and crumpled to the ground like a wet piece of paper. He scooped her up in his arms and brushed the sand off her face.

"Come off the ground, my daughter. That isn't where you belong. Shh, there's no need to cry. I love you so much. Please don't cry." He held her to his chest and reassured her his love would be there until the end.

I ran my hand through my sweaty hair and paced back to the shore. It didn't surprise me to hear Gwendolyn committed murder. In an ocean where territory was a precious commodity, such actions were perfectly acceptable. Murder didn't only happen in the ocean, it happened often. Truth be known, the act wasn't even called murder amongst merfolk, but the foolish breach of unspoken code. Not to mention the myriad of other reasons that would conjure such a violent response. For the life of a mermaid was a continual ebb and flow of heartless insanity, but the ways of humans were much more civilized. They valued the lives of each other and punished those who didn't.

I looked back at Mr. Hart who clung to his daughter in adoration. His face was flushed and swollen from crying. He made eye contact with me and smiled as if he knew I heard the conversation the whole time. I felt my face grow hot, and I looked the other way. It didn't surprise me to hear Gwendolyn committed murder—it surprised me to hear her father still loved her after knowing she committed it.

She suddenly broke from their embrace and sputtered a throaty cough. Her face changed from ivory to purple as she gasped desperately for air. Mr. Hart looked at me and nodded in an unspoken confirmation of our previous arrangement. I glanced down at my watch and calculated the minutes since she surfaced. Her time on the land was running out. Something had to be done so she could breathe.

He asked if she was feeling okay and she nodded, suppressing a cough with the back of her hand. After a few seconds of her gathering her composure, she smiled with words of reassurance and leaned back on his chest. The father wrapped his arms around his daughter and wiped his brow with a tissue. He appeared to be anxious. His wide eyes darted from mine to the top of Gwendolyn's head. The purpose of his arrival had finally come.

I turned in the direction of the ocean and walked to the water's edge. Gwendolyn's meeting with her father was only the beginning. They were going to walk from the shore and make new memories as a family. I smiled at the thought of them driving home and pushed my hands in my pockets. A small part of my soul felt at peace. Yes, I was the cause of Gwendolyn's catastrophic transformation, but I found the solution to see her through. She wasn't going to have to kill a man to become a human. Just knowing that I saved a life gave me such hope.

A large wave spread across the sand, leaving a glowing shell in its sweeping foam. I bent to the ground and picked up a perfectly round sand dollar. Who would have ever foreseen such a change of tides would take place? Within the same night, I wished for death and valued life. Within the same night, I questioned grace and saw it given. Within the same night, I carried regrets and let them go. I slipped the shell in my pocket and chuckled quietly to myself. Perhaps it was a little token of a night of new beginnings.

A high-pitched scream rang out from behind me.

The hair on the back of my neck stood on end. I spun around and fell to my knees in horror.

Gwendolyn sat alone in a pile of ash.

Chapter Fourteen

"I don't know what happened! He didn't kiss my lips! He never kissed my lips! Oh, Marcus, help me! Dear, God, help me! He's gone! He's gone!" I looked down at the remains of what was left of my father and grasped two fistfuls of ash. "This can't be! How can this be? He never kissed my lips! I don't understand what's happening right now!" I wailed in sheer despondency and wiped the ash on the sand. The black powder smeared like paint.

Marcus stood from his knelt position on the shore and ran to where I sat. He pushed his hair out of his eyes and paced the ground like an animal. "Oh, Gwendolyn, I'm sorry. I'm so sorry." The fervent mumble that resembled an apology transitioned to a torrent of obscenities. He kicked at the sand in an outpouring of wrath. "Curse the gods! Curse the sun and moon! I'm so sorry. This wasn't supposed to happen like this. He . . . I mean . . . he wasn't supposed to die. I was hoping he . . ." He looked up at the sky and shook his fist.

I spread my hands in his direction. "He was just holding me and then he vanished. He kissed the top of my head, but he never kissed my lips. That's not how someone gives their soul, is it? So, why did he turn to ash?!" I beat at the ground until the sand broke my skin and sobbed hysterically. It all felt like some nightmare I couldn't wake up from. I held my sides and rocked back and forth to keep from processing the moment. "Please, Dad. Please, Dad. Please come back. Please come back. Please come back . . ." My voice was talking, but it sounded muffled and distorted. I felt as though I was losing control. "Please, Dad. Please, Dad. Please." A ringing in my ears signaled I was going to faint.

Marcus broke from his internal struggle and knelt to the ground before me. He grasped my hands and applied firm pressure to steady my body that shook. Although my eyes were filled with tears, I could see he was beat up from his own demons. His thumbs softly stroked mine. "I'm so sorry you lost your father. I can't imagine the pain you must be feeling. I wish I could take it all from you and bear some of the hurt myself." He turned his face toward the ground and cursed under his breath. "I should've never gotten involved. This wasn't supposed to end like this. I was hoping I found another way." He whispered he was sorry and continued to rub my hands.

My eyes wandered to the woolen coat and trousers that lay crumpled in our presence. I could still feel their scratchy material as my father hugged me to his chest. His coat was damp and covered with sand—probably caused from him standing at the tide pools as he waited for my arrival. I choked on the tears that threatened to pour and tore my vision from the garments. "How can this not be my fault? My father would be here right now if it wasn't for me. I killed him, Marcus. How am I supposed to live with myself?"

He gave my hands a tight squeeze. "You can't blame yourself for something you didn't do. Look at me. You didn't know this was going to happen. Did you? How could this be your fault? You didn't kill him."

I stretched my tail that was beginning to feel dry and flipped it to its moist side. My father didn't even question my form. He never made me feel weird or out of place. I never needed to explain why I looked different. He just saw that I was his daughter and knew I needed help. Such an unequivocal love was impossible to accept.

"If I didn't transform, he would've never given his life. I took him from this world, and I don't know how else to see it. And this tail . . . this repulsive tail . . . it's my fault. All of it." I buried my face in my hands and released a flood of anguish. The ash on my palms mixed with the tears on my cheeks and burned my eyes—a stinging reminder of the consequence of my trespass.

"No!" Marcus barked, pulling from his perturbed state. He quickly stripped off his shirt and wiped my face with it. "Your father gave his life by choice! He knew what it would take to transform you into a human, and he did so willingly. It wasn't an accident. He wasn't caught off guard. You never murdered him because he made that choice himself." He cleaned another smear off my cheek and twisted his shirt into a tight ball. He threw it into a spreading wave and sighed.

"It's my fault," he said bleakly. He looked for my reaction and broke eye contact. "I remembered the promise I made to you on the night we kissed, and I wanted to be a man of my word. I told you I would find another way to release you from this . . . this hell," he snarled, motioning toward the ocean. "I heard once that a perfect sacrifice of love would spare a victim from giving their life. And I couldn't think of a more pure love than that of your father. Looking back, it was a foolish idea. I really didn't think it through. I didn't consider the risk he was taking and how it would affect you."

Marcus's eyes wandered back to my face and softened. He was expecting to see me angry with his rash choices, but I wasn't. I was devastated about the loss of my father, but I couldn't charge him with wrongdoing. He had gone to the ends of the earth to keep me from murdering. He didn't want me to experience the regret he suffered. As I looked at his face that was marred with remorse, I felt a deep sympathy for his life. He was a lost, despairing individual in need of a compass. He was blind, groping in the darkness, yet he was willing to find my way. I couldn't be more thankful.

Why did he still care for me?

"When I explained your situation to your father, he agreed to help you without any hesitation. But before I could stop him, he —"

I clutched my stomach and groaned. My body broke out into a cold sweat that appeared out of the middle of nowhere. A dull cramp gripped the middle of my waist and spread down the length of my tail.

Marcus's eyes widened. He jumped to a stand and nearly tripped over his feet. "Gosh! I can't believe I almost forgot.

I'll be right back. Hang on for me." He ran to the formation of rocks behind us and reappeared with a bright purple
backpack. His shaky hands fumbled eagerly with the zipper
as he pulled out a pink beach towel and a familiar pair of
sweats. He set my clothes on the sand and reached to hold
my hand. "This is going to hurt for only a moment. When
it's finished, you'll have your legs. I'll be right here."

I could barely hear him through the searing pain. The
cramp that started as a dull throb pierced deeper with every
breath I took. I squeezed his hand, but released it with another
moan. The skin of my waist prickled with a sensation of
crawling worms. Their movement intensified as the pain
transferred through flesh and muscle, spreading deep into
my bones. I fell to the sand and writhed in sheer agony.

"I'm right here. It's going to be over soon. You're doing
great."

My tail involuntarily pulsed and quivered as the severance
of bone and tissue began to take place. A small tear formed
between my fins. The narrow split bled as it widened and
divided, cutting through my tail to the bottom half of my
torso. I filled my lungs with a deep breath of air and let out a
blood-curdling scream. I no longer had one tail that flapped
in the sand, but two.

"It's almost over, Gwendolyn. It's almost over."

My body racked violently as sinews of muscle and tissue
formed the curve of thighs. Two large bones connected to
sockets, and the angular bend of knees took their shape.

I'm so sorry . . .

The length of muscle and bones narrowed to shins. The
delicate width of ankles appeared.

I'm so sorry, Dad.

My split fins filled with flesh. Two nubs swelled to form heels and ten toes separated. The greenish-gray scales that freckled my torso vanished to ivory skin.

I saw my father. He yelled my name with a voice that could be heard over the waves and ran across the sand to meet me. We clung to each other and wept. He said he prayed for me every night since my disappearance and was overjoyed to see I was okay. I broke from our embrace and spread my hands across my tail. I was painfully aware of my fish's appendage that looked so different from his legs. My father, noticing my embarrassment, shook his head with a smile and leaned to my ear. "My love will be enough."

I wiped the tears that ran down my cheeks and slowly opened my eyes. The moon that hung in the star-speckled sky shone with less clarity. The sand beneath my body felt sharp, and I could no longer taste the sorrow that leaked from Marcus's heart, but the salty sea air that blew across my skin. The world around me changed from my new human's point of view. My transformation was complete. The curse that crippled my life for seven months had finally lifted. No longer did I need to bear the burden of worrying about killing a man because my father died for me. I looked down at my legs that glowed under the stars and gave a silent cry.

"I'm so sorry," Marcus whispered. He draped the towel across my waist and set the folded sweats near my head. I propped up both elbows, and he turned away to offer privacy. "I can't say 'I'm sorry' enough. I just wish things were different. You should've never transformed into a mermaid. None of this would've happened if I didn't tell you about

Ryan. I should've stayed out of it from the beginning . . . I should've taken your place."

I felt my eyes grow wide. I never thought about Marcus's fate until now. If he led my father to the shore to give his life, was he going to suffer the traitor's curse, too? I took a wobbly stand and put on my pants with shaky hands. "What about you? Are you going to fall under the traitor's curse because you led my father to his . . . to his . . ." I bit my lower lip and pulled the drawstring of my sweats. I couldn't bring myself to finish my sentence. I stripped off the wetsuit that clung to me like a disease and reached for my fleecy top.

He scratched the back of his neck and sat on his haunches. The night around us grew still as he pondered my question for a moment. He muttered a mouthful of obscenities and shrugged his shoulders. "I didn't think about that. I suppose I could be cursed. As I said, I really didn't think about what could happen. I wasn't expecting for your father to die. Well, I mean, I thought about it for a second. But when I saw the love he had for you, I dispelled any doubt in my mind. How could his offering not be enough? He didn't hesitate to give you everything he had. That has to mean something, doesn't it? I mean, how can his sacrifice be the same as some lust-filled meat-head giving his soul?" He took in a deep breath and released it loudly. "Your father followed me out here with a purpose. He didn't just want to see you again—he wanted to save you. He kissed the top of your head because he wanted to give you his life. I just don't see how that's not enough."

I sat down next to him and reached to hold his hand. He flinched at my touch, but he didn't pull away. "I don't understand any of this either," I murmured. I swallowed the lump that burned in my throat and shook my head. "I'm so sorry if you transform again. This all seems so wrong."

I hung my head between my knees and stared at the broken shells in the sand. Our lives seemed a lot like the pearlescent fragments. Perhaps our futures held promise at some point in time, but the decisions we made shattered those promises. They shattered the people around us. Marcus was going to possibly suffer on the account of me. He had unknowingly thrown away his future for someone who treated him like trash. The more I considered the precious lives that were strewn in my wake, the more I couldn't live with myself. My world would no longer feel the same without my father. Every time I smiled, every time I laughed, every time I embraced someone with love and affection; I would remember the life that was given for mine.

I cringed as a new pain punched me right in the stomach. For the first time in the night, I realized something that I haven't thought of before.

My mother was widowed.

I let out a cry and blinked, sending two tears streaming toward the sand. I quickly wiped my face and tried my best to smile. "I don't know why things are so messed up right now. But I'm here for you, Marcus. I'll be right here if you transform. I can come out every night and keep you company. We can meet at the tide pools, if you want. I'll try my best to help you in any way I can."

He looked up from the ground and cocked his head to one side. "Really? I wasn't expecting to hear you say that. I guess it won't be so bad then. I don't know, the thought of not dealing with traffic anymore is pretty cool." We made eye contact and burst out laughing. It was the first time I truly laughed in months.

"I hate getting trapped behind buses when I need to be somewhere. Actually, it will be nice to not have to deal with Avangeline anymore. I can't wait to get her out of my apartment. I'm sure it will throw her for a loop that I'm gone. And that's not a bad thing."

"You're being such a good sport about all of this," I said, dropping my arm from his shoulders. I wanted to hold his hand, but I refrained. "I'm so sorry you got involved. I would feel horrible if something happened to you."

"Please don't apologize anymore. This isn't your fault. It's just the way things happened to play out." He stretched his long legs out in front of himself and crossed his feet. He stared at the waves that spread before us and cleared his throat. "So, how long after Avangeline transformed did you . . . transform, too?"

I turned toward the horseshoe cluster of rocks as my mind replayed the events of that night. It seemed like only yesterday that Ryan died in the arms of Avangeline. I shuddered at the memory and looked at Marcus. "I really don't know for sure. It all happened so fast. I remember watching her get dressed. You stepped out from the rocks, and she talked to you for a bit. Maybe a few minutes, or so?"

Marcus looked down at his legs as if he was expecting for his transformation to happen at that very moment. I reached to hold his hand and smoothed it.

"It's going to be okay. I'll be right here for you. We'll get through this together."

He nodded with a forced smile. "Thanks. I'll be okay. I guess I'll just have to sweat it out then." He drew his knees to his chest and rested his chin on them.

We sat together without saying another word as we anxiously waited for his end to begin. A spreading wave reached my wetsuit and covered it. The blanket of water pulled back from the sand, taking the abominable garment with it. A sea turtle bobbed and surfaced with the foam. She shuffled across the sand with a sense of urgency and stopped to dig a hole. Every few minutes, Marcus would look from his watch, to his legs, and then back to the ocean. He took in a deep breath and let it out with a sputter.

"Well, I guess that's it!" he announced, jumping to his feet. He reached for my hand and pulled me to a stand. "I guess I have to still deal with Avangeline's annoying voice after all. I don't know why I was spared from the curse. Maybe it had to do with my intentions or something. I don't know. But whatever it is, I'm not complaining." He opened my backpack and began to stuff my father's clothes into it.

I grimaced at the image and focused on the tumbling waves. I thanked my father for his sacrifice and whispered my goodbyes.

"Are you ready to go? I can drive you home, if you want."

"Yes," I said, closing my eyes. I wiped the tear that ran down my cheek and reached to hold his hand. "Thank you."

We looked at the ocean one last time and started for the parking lot. The moon provided plenty of light as we navigated through the driftwood that was scattered across the sand. I tripped on a rock that hid in a patch of moss, and Marcus helped me up.

"Hello?" A familiar voice called from behind us.

I spun around and squinted toward the shore. The silhouette of a man walked in our direction.

"Can you two spare me a towel?"

I clasped my hand over my mouth and looked up at Marcus.

He found a way.

Tides of Souls

The Unspoken Heart Series

Marcus opened the door of his car and led me out by the hand. His arms circled around my waist as he drew me to himself. He whispered I was beautiful and leaned in to give me a kiss. The heady smell of leather and cedarwood made my heart pound.

"I'll never grow tired of doing that," he uttered, caressing my cheeks with his thumbs. His eyes studied mine for a moment and crinkled with a smile. "I have to pinch myself sometimes to remember this isn't a dream." He gave me another kiss and reached to hold my hand. He closed the door behind me and beeped his car's alarm.

"I'll never get tired of this either," I sighed, weaving my fingers between his. Marcus had a way of stirring the unspoken emotions of my heart. In the three months since I became human, we developed a relationship that never had a chance to flourish. I helped him fight his inner demons while he helped me battle mine. He never pointed fingers or cast judgement. He chose not to mention the past that haunted me in my dreams. He treated me with a genuine kindness that I never experienced with anyone else. Even my father approved of our relationship.

Our enraptured stroll slowly came to an end as we entered La Mer's full parking lot. He let go of my hand and walked a few steps ahead of me. "I don't get it," he said, looking around the dimly lit lot. He scratched the back of his head as if he was unfamiliar with where he was. "I know it's been a while since I actually stepped foot in this place, but the staff couldn't have changed that much. I don't recognize any of these cars." He mumbled something about seeing Lance's truck and frowned. "These can't be customers because the club hasn't opened yet."

"How long has it been since you were here?" I asked, pulling my cardigan sweater closed. The night's cool breeze picked up, and I smoothed back my hair behind my ears.

He muttered a comment about his absence being foolish and cursed. "I've been here, but I haven't really cared. Are you wondering how long it's been since I've actually managed the place? I don't know. Maybe a few months, or so? The club has been running on autopilot since you transformed into a mermaid. Well, autopilot and Avangeline's help. Which isn't a good thing. Let's just hope she hasn't painted the walls hot pink or something." He chuckled with nervous energy and reached for my hand again.

I craned my neck and pointed to the street. "Maybe the employees are parked somewhere else? Down GlenPoint Strip maybe? Is it possible that Avangeline hired a bunch of new people and these are their cars?"

We walked to the back of the building and stopped under a lamppost. He pulled his keys out from his pocket and turned around so he could give me his full attention. A muscle in his jaw clenched. "I certainly hope she hasn't hired anyone. I never gave her the authority to do that. Can you imagine how her decisions could destroy my business? How could she be a good judge of character if she isn't a good character herself?" He shook his head with another obscenity and unlocked the door of the club. He allowed for me to walk in front of him, and we both stepped inside.

I paused and blinked as my eyes adjusted to the candle-light that flickered across the room. La Mer remained as I remembered it. Thick tapestries of purple and scarlet covered the tall, twelve-foot walls. There were tables with chairs and golden pillows, and the exotic smell of food and incense was near intoxicating. We stood at the front podium and waited to be noticed. For as many cars that were parked in the lot, there was only one woman that was visible from where we stood. She crossed the room with a sense of urgency.

"I'm sorry, we're not open yet. Can I help you?"

"Yes. I'd like to get a table in the back of the room please, Kyla. Is that how you pronounce your name? Any table that offers privacy will do."

The gorgeous woman with glossy black hair reached for her nametag. Frustration flickered across her face as she entertained Marcus's oblivious request. She fluttered her eyelashes and continued to stare as if she was waiting for him to say he was joking. He remained silent. Her red lips pursed in a sneer.

"Yes, that's how you pronounce my name. But didn't you hear what I just said? We're not open yet. I can't seat you." Her long fingernails tapped out a rhythm on the podium.

Marcus smiled and reached for a menu on the table. "Sure. I heard you say you're not open. But your hours don't pertain to us. Please excuse me for not introducing myself right away. My name is Marcus, and I'm the owner of La Mer. I'd like to be seated in the back of the room, if that's okay with you. If not, I can just pick the table myself. I suppose it's out of an abundance of courtesy that I stopped to talk to you in the first place."

The hostess's cheeks turned bright pink. I couldn't tell if she was angry or embarrassed. She mumbled a quick apology and turned around to lead us through the club. Marcus looked at me and winked as we made our way past the dancefloor to a shadowed table in the back of the room. I stiffened at the familiar location and released his hand with a gasp. The booth that Marcus sat in when I gave him my invitation was directly in front of our table. He noticed my discomfort and turned around.

"We don't have to sit here," he whispered, giving the hostess his back. She rolled her eyes and held her hips in annoyance. "I'm sorry for any memories that come to mind. I can tear down this booth tomorrow, if you want me to. It means nothing to me." He turned to Kyla and pointed across the room. "Kyla, this table won't work for us. We need to be seated in the lounge area." He motioned to a location near the entrance and looked at me for approval.

I shook my head and reached for his hands. "No, it's okay. I'm sorry if I showed any displeasure. This table will do just fine. We can make a new memory here." I forced myself to smile, and he nodded in agreement. He escorted me to my chair and pushed it in when I sat. The infuriated hostess saw that she was no longer needed and turned to walk away.

"Hey, Kyla?"

"Yes?"

"Try to smile a little. You're in the business of hospitality."

She looked at Marcus and smirked with a mouthful of daggers. We watched as she sauntered across the club and disappeared behind the servers' station. Marcus looked at me and pretended to strangle his neck.

"Wow. I take it you didn't hire her."

"No, I didn't. And if she's the face of my business, I'll be out of business. She'll drive everyone away." His eyes narrowed on a waitress who entered the room with a tray. He reached across the table and held both of my hands. "Hey, listen," he said, stroking my fingers with his thumbs. "I'm really sorry for what happened when I sat at that booth. I was such a creep back then. I had so much to learn about life and how to treat people. There isn't a day that goes by that I haven't wished to do things over . . . especially that night. I shouldn't have held you there against your will. And those two women that you saw me sitting with . . . well, I wasn't with—"

I lifted my hand to stop him. "Please don't say anymore. I really don't need any explanations. I accept you for who you are. You don't have to worry about your past—just as I don't have to worry about mine. We both have things we would rather forget, right? Just as long as you aren't seeing those women now or anything."

He shook his head fervently. "No. No! You're it, Gwendolyn. You're it. My heart is totally yours."

I smiled and smoothed my hand over his. "Good, because my heart is yours, too."

Another server appeared and sat at a nearby table to fold napkins. Marcus watched him intently. "I don't recognize him," he said under his breath. The unknown waiter looked up from his napkins to talk to a waitress that entered the room. She sat down next to him and started to fold. "I don't recognize any of them. Something isn't right about all of this. If anything, they certainly need better training. Half the tables haven't even been set yet. And Kyla . . . well, I don't know for sure, but I think she's—"

"Hello, folks, my name is Shannon. I'll be your server today."

I looked up at the woman who appeared out of the middle of nowhere and nearly toppled out of my chair. The waitress was stunning. Her sandy blonde hair fell past her shoulders in a cloud of perfectly soft waves. Her face was adorned with high cheekbones and pink full lips. She smiled in my direction, and I nervously looked away. Perhaps I felt intimidated because Marcus could have any woman he wanted. His charisma could seduce the prettiest female in the building, and she was most certainly a contender! I just couldn't compete. He gave my hands a reassuring squeeze.

"Can I start you both off with something to drink tonight? How about an iced tea or a chardonnay? We have a pretty impressive wine menu, if you'd like to take a look . . ."

Marcus promptly shook his head. "No alcohol. But I'd love some ice water. Do you want anything to drink, Gwendolyn? No? We'll both have water for now." He looked at me and gave a wink.

"Great, okay. Two ice waters," Shannon repeated, writing on her notepad. She looked at our menu that was tucked under a napkin and frowned. "Did you both get a chance to take a look at the menu yet? Our specials tonight are cedar-plank halibut over a bed of wild greens, lamb rack with a parsley crust, and duck confit."

"You're serving duck confit now?" Marcus questioned, raising an eyebrow. "Wow. That's a pretty ambitious dish. I didn't know Lance wanted to explore such a complicated recipe. Well, I guess I'll have to try that then. Do you still serve oysters on the half shell? Let's start with an order of those, too." He glanced at me and winced with a chuckle. "Gosh, how rude of me to order first. I'm sorry. What would you like to eat? Do you need a few minutes to take a look at the menu?"

"Do you offer anything vegetarian?" I asked, clearing my throat with a cough. I made eye contact with the waitress and looked past her. A few workers were setting up a grouping of candles near a curtained wall.

Shannon smiled and nodded. "Yes. We make a delicious vegetable wellington served with wild rice. We also have spinach pasta and cauliflower steamed in white wine."

"The vegetable wellington sounds great. I think I'll try that."

She nodded and scribbled. "Sure. Vegetable wellington is a perfect choice. Okay, I'll make sure to get that appetizer of oysters out as soon as possible. And I'll be back with your drinks. Just let me get that menu first . . ." She reached across the table to take the laminated placard.

Marcus's eyes narrowed as she leaned in. "Shannon?"

"Yes?"

"How long have you been working here?

"A few months, I think. Why?"

"I'm just curious. I haven't seen you before. Who hired you? If you don't mind me asking."

"I don't mind. I interviewed with Avangeline. She hires everyone who works here."

"Really?" Marcus's eyes dilated to complete black. *"Is she working tonight?"*

The beautiful woman with long blonde hair stiffened. She dropped her pen and stooped to the ground to pick it up.

"It's okay. I don't care what you are or where you came from. I just need to know if Avangeline is working tonight. I would like to talk to her as soon as possible."

"Yes, she's in her office. I'll let her know you want to speak to her." She lifted to a stand and adjusted her apron. Marcus thanked her and she smiled, but she looked like she wanted to cry. I quickly stripped off my sweater and slung it on the back of my chair. I was beginning to feel sorry for her.

"I'll go get those waters for you. If you'll excuse me, I'll be on my way."

I looked up at Marcus when I was sure she was gone and slowly shook my head. His face was creased in a scowl.

"I don't know why Avangeline would hire a mermaid. It just doesn't make any sense. I had this place all buttoned up when I left it with her. This club was running like a well-oiled machine. Why would she want to complicate things by taking matters into her own hands?"

A busboy excused himself for interrupting our conversation and set down our waters with a bow. Marcus's eyes widened when he left.

"He's one, too? Bloody hell! What's going on here? This whole room is crawling with them!" His finger pointed around the room. "She's one. He's one. He's one. She's one. Kyla's one. Curse this whole place! Everyone working here is one!" He took a long drink from his water and set it down with a slam. He folded his hands across the table and drew in a deep breath. The tragedy of the night's unveiling was slowly setting in.

"My club is ruined," he said finally. He stretched his long legs out from under the table and hooked his hands behind his head. "Everything I've worked for is gone. I played the fool to madness and folly and handed my business over to a snake. I'm going to have to fire everyone in the building and close my doors for an indefinite amount of time. My reputation will probably take weeks to recover." He pulled on the collar of his shirt and cursed Avangeline's existence.

I reached for his hand and tried my best to smile. "Aww, come on. It can't be that bad. Why do you have to fire everyone just because they're mermaids? Surely there has to be some good found in merfolk."

Marcus shook his head and took another sip from his glass. "No. I don't mean to sound rude, but no. There's never any good to be found in merfolk. And if there is, I wouldn't know how to find it. How do you take a roomful of heartless people and try to figure out if they want one? It would be easier for me to just fire everyone and—" He stopped mid-sentence and turned as white as his shirt. I turned my head to see what he was staring at and covered my mouth with a gasp. The curtains that hung from the wall were drawn and a very large painting extended its length.

It was a painting of Avangeline.

Her fiery red hair was unmistakable, but it was the way she was painted that made me cringe in repulsion. She was painted in her mermaid form. Candles were arranged below the picture, making it appear to be a kind of shrine.

Just at that moment, the door of the club opened and a worker carrying flowers entered the room. He paused to look at the painting and lowered to one knee to pay his respects. He arranged the flowers around the candles and slowly took a stand.

Marcus sputtered out his water. "What the heck is going on here?!" He jumped to his feet, and I coaxed him to sit down. He punched the table with the side of his fist, and a fork fell to the ground. "Did he just bow before that painting? And is that supposed to be Avangeline? I'm grateful there's an age limit to enter this place because she has all of her body parts hanging out." He threatened to kick everyone out of the building and punched the table again. "How dare she? How dare she do this without me knowing? She's turned my club into a bloody circus!"

A few workers turned in our direction. I tried to quiet him down, but he wouldn't listen.

"No! I won't be stopped! I've had enough of Avangeline's foolish antics. Who does she think she is? A god? Does she really think she can take over my club? This city? She's got another thing coming to her if she thinks she does. I tell you the truth, I've had enough. Enough! She's out! I'm kicking her out tonight!"

I suddenly wished we were closer to the entrance. We could slip out the door and have our conversation in private.

A brisk walk through the parking lot could help him let off some steam. A handful of servers appeared from the servers' station and joined the ones who were staring. We all at once became the spectacle of the whole room. Marcus seemed oblivious to their presence.

"I should've never let her in. Hell, what a mistake I made. I was such a moron to let her take control. If only I had left her on the shore to figure out her own future. She wouldn't have ruined mine. She wouldn't . . . have . . . She wouldn't have . . . have . . ." He wiped his face with a napkin and blinked. "She wouldn't have ruined mine." He looked at me and winced. His face was pale and sweaty.

"Marcus? Are you okay? Listen, we'll get through this. At least she didn't paint the walls hot pink, right? It's just a painting. You can take it down. You can fire all the workers that don't have any ethics and take control again. Nothing is broken that can't be fixed here. I promise. You'll get your club back. It will just take a little work, that's all. I can help you pick up the pieces."

He nodded, but his expression remained vacant. He swayed slightly in his chair.

"Gwendolyn, I don't feel good. Something isn't right."

"What do you mean?"

"I feel dizzy. It's like I'm drunk . . . really drunk, actually. I think I'm going to pass out."

"What? Here . . ." I pushed his glass of water to his hand. "Take another drink. You're probably going into shock. Everything will be okay. I promise. Come on, drink it slowly and count to three. Or maybe hold your head between your knees and take a deep breath. I know when I feel dizzy, I—"

He flung his arm across the table and knocked my glass to the floor. Water and silverware spilled into my lap. I gasped and jumped to my feet.

"Don't drink the water! Run! Get out of here before it's too late!" He clutched his stomach and groaned that it hurt. I reached across the table to give him my hand, but he didn't reach for it. He slid off his chair and crumpled to the floor.

My face broke out in a cold sweat. I grabbed my purse and spun around to look for help. My knee slammed against my chair, and I toppled over it.

"So, I see you made it out of the ocean in one piece," a woman's voice called. "What a pity I wasn't there to stop it from happening."

I untangled from the legs of my chair and painfully rose to my feet. My skin prickled with gooseflesh as I looked around the dark room. The workers that watched us from the shadows had surrounded our table in a large semicircle. One of them took a step forward.

"This one suffered the traitor's curse, everyone," Avangeline announced. She looked at Marcus and muttered a crude comment. "And the imbecile lying on the ground is her follower. He calls himself the owner of this club, but don't listen to him. He obviously doesn't know what he's talking about." She looked at Kyla and shook her head. "Does he really look like a man with authority to you?"

The room began to murmur in response. I spotted an opening in their tight-knit huddle and pushed through them for the exit. A hand grabbed me by my arm and pulled me back to the table. I turned around and nearly stifled a scream.

"Hello, Gwendolyn," Sabrina cooed. She released my arm with a push and giggled when I ran into a table. "Wow. What are the chances of us meeting here on land? I'm surprised to see you finally met someone to break your traitor's curse." Her eyes narrowed on my legs and then looked down to her own. She pulled on the hem of her short red dress and fluffed her hair. "It didn't take me very long to get my legs either. My last encounter was surprisingly quick. I did make sure to give Joey your regards before I took his soul." She said something about his hair being another color, and Avangeline laughed.

Sabrina's face grew suddenly serious. "The last time you and I talked, you told me to find a new territory. I was already planning to take the pier, so I really didn't care. But I've thought about that conversation ever since we parted. I imagined how good it would feel to tell you the same thing. Well, as the gods would have it, here's my opportunity." She looked to the back of the room and called for someone named Isaiah. "Gwendolyn, this territory isn't working out for you anymore. I think you better go."

Before I knew what was happening, a large man grabbed me by my upper arm and escorted me out the exit. He shoved me to the pavement and closed the door behind me. The pain I felt from falling on the asphalt paled in comparison to the pain of knowing Marcus was left in the building.

I looked up at the starless sky and muttered a feeble prayer for help. Heaven only knew how I would get him back.

Amy Astorga has a passion for unearthing monsters that lurk in the darkness and illuminating their pathways to redemption. Unafraid to take chances, she boldly fuses dark fantasy with powerful, faith-based themes. Her narratives point readers toward a transcendent hope only found in Christ.

When she's not navigating the beautiful chaos of raising six children, Amy can be found collecting perfumes, studying insects, or losing a battle with a never-ending pile of laundry.

Follow amyastorga.com for updates.